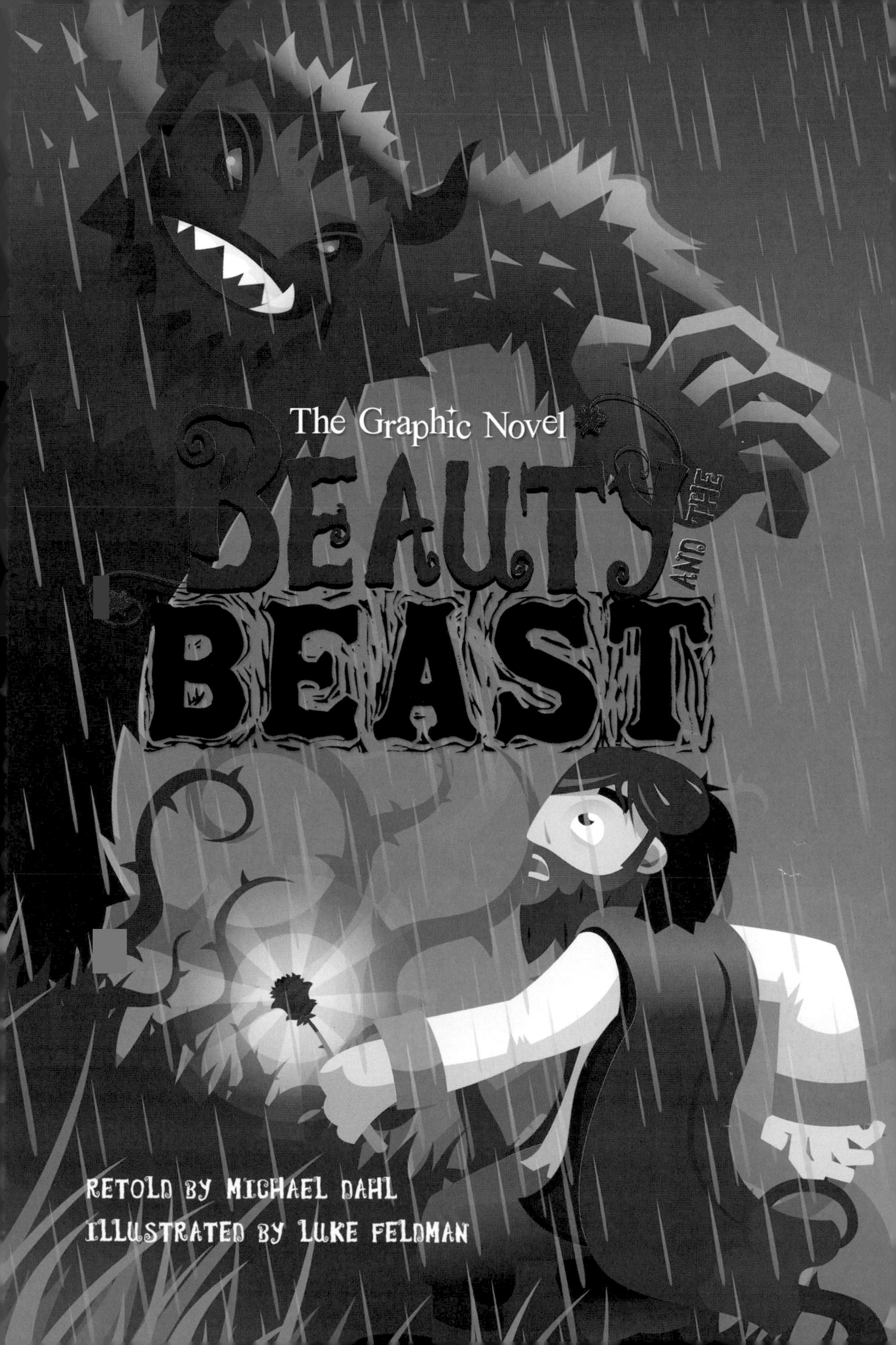
The Graphic Novel
BEAUTY AND THE BEAST
RETOLD BY MICHAEL DAHL
ILLUSTRATED BY LUKE FELDMAN

Graphic Spin is published by Stone Arch Books
A Capstone Imprint
1710 Roe Crest Drive
North Mankato, Minnesota 56003
www.capstonepub.com

Library of Congress Cataloging-in-Publication Data
Dahl, Michael.
    Beauty and the Beast: The Graphic Novel / retold by Michael Dahl; illustrated by Luke
Feldman.
    p. cm. — (Graphic Spin)
    ISBN 978-1-4342-0765-4 (library binding)
    ISBN 978-1-4342-0861-3 (pbk.)
    1. Graphic novels. [1. Graphic novels. 2. Fairy tales. 3. Folklore—France.] I. Feldman, Luke, ill.
II. Beauty and the beast. English. III. Title.
PZ7.7.D14Be 2009
[Fic]—dc22   2008006719

Summary: In a dark forest, a merchant picks a rose for his daughter Beauty. It belongs to a terrible
beast. To save his life, the merchant promises that his daughter will visit the creature. When she does,
Beauty grows to like the beast. But can she ever love him?

Art Director: Heather Kindseth
Graphic Designer: Kay Fraser

Librarian Reviewer
Katharine Kan
Graphic novel reviewer and Library Consultant, Panama City, FL
MLS in Library and Information Studies, University of Hawaii at Manoa, HI

Reading Consultant
Elizabeth Stedem
Educator/Consultant, Colorado Springs, CO
MA in Elementary Education, University of Denver, CO

Printed in the United States of America in Stevens Point, Wisconsin.
112011
006489R

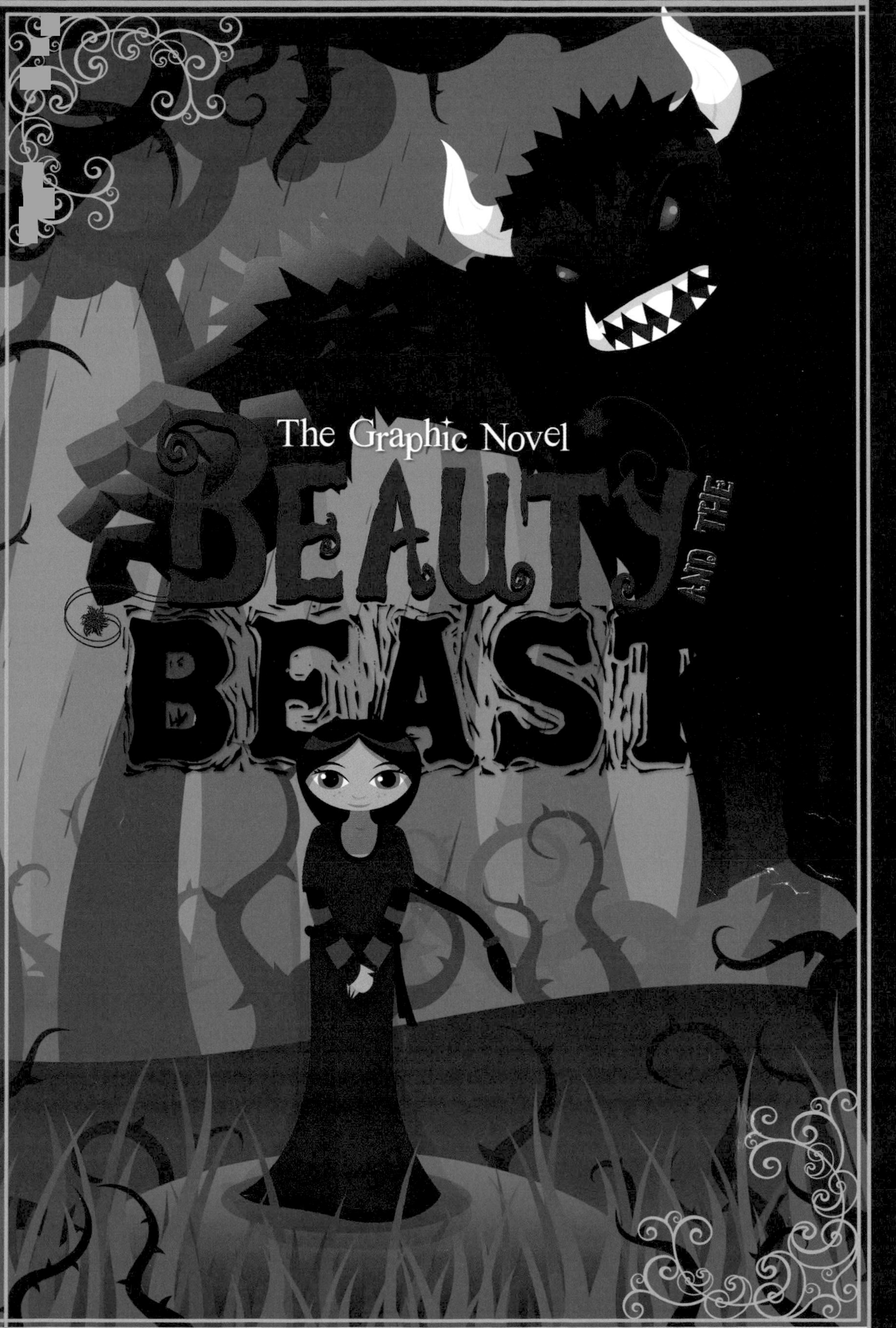
The Graphic Novel
BEAUTY AND THE BEAST

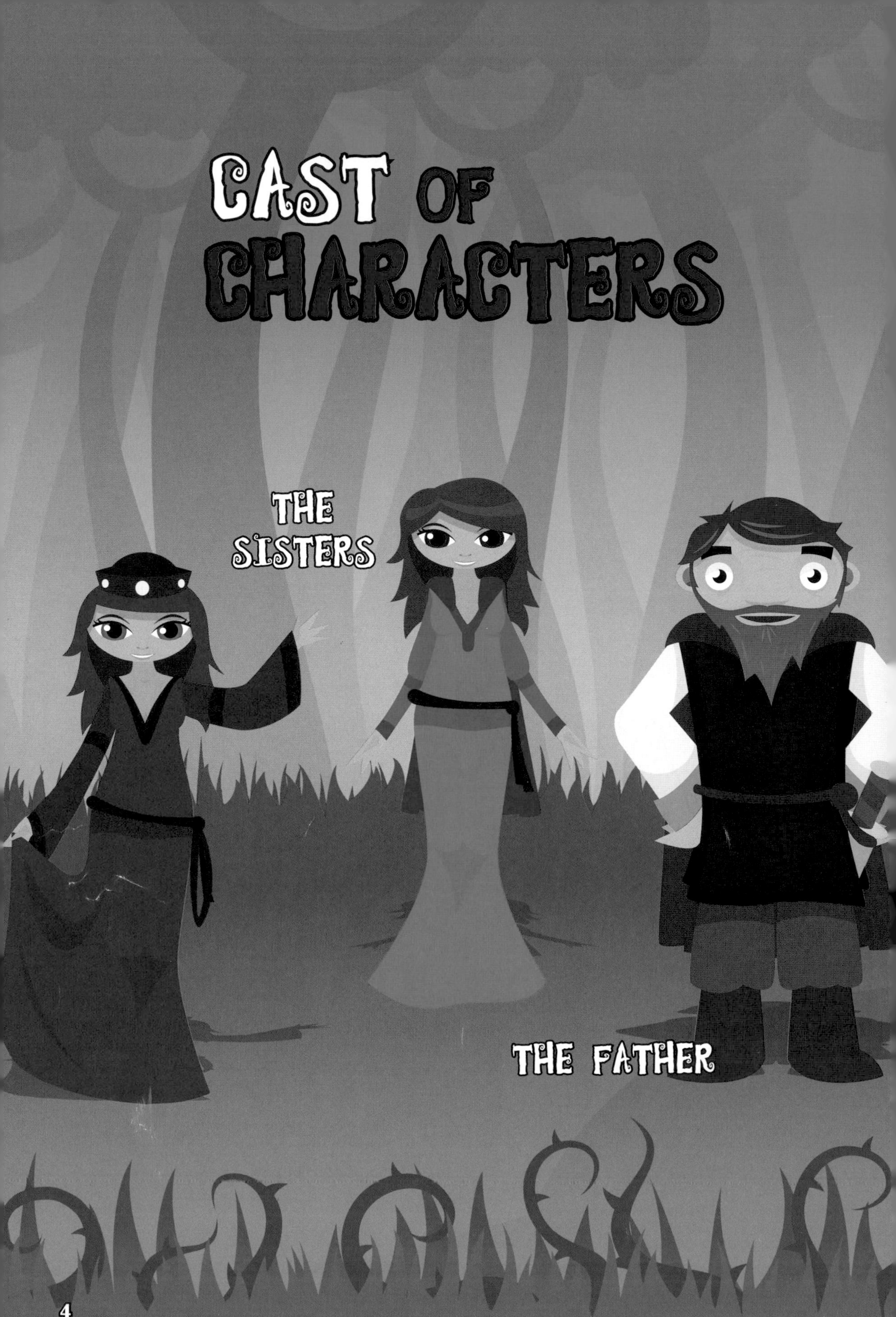
CAST OF CHARACTERS
THE SISTERS
THE FATHER

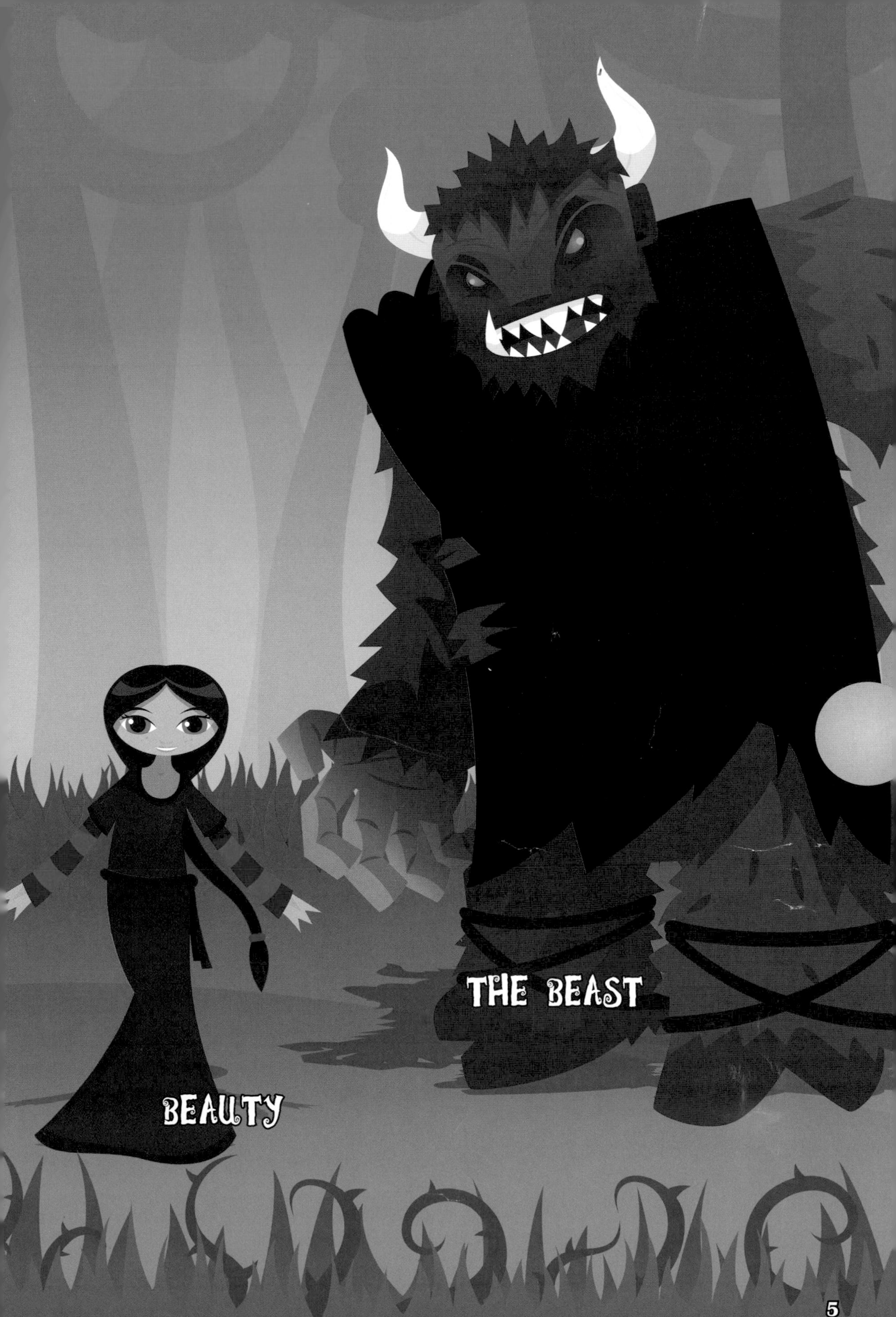
THE BEAST
BEAUTY

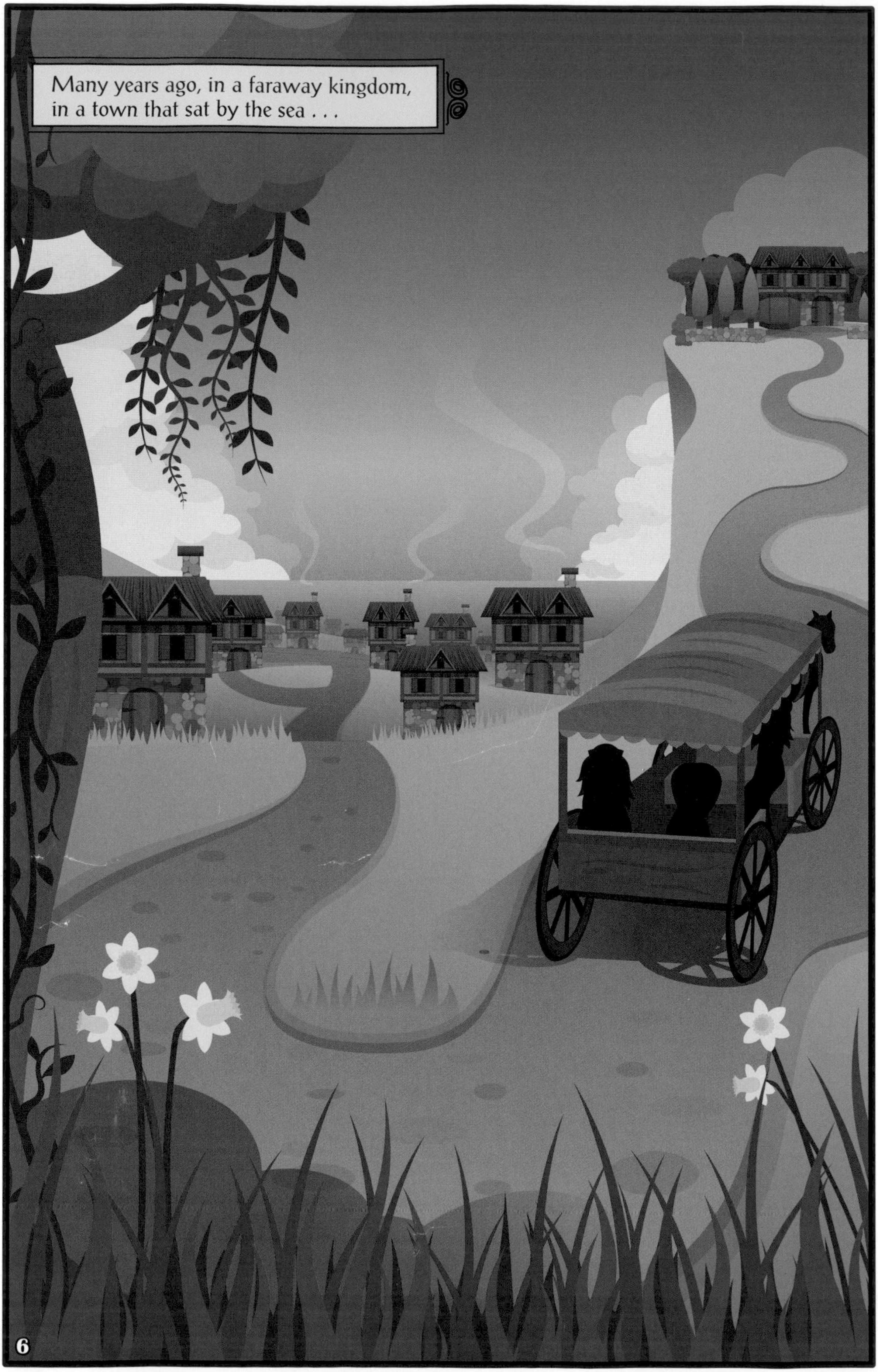
Many years ago, in a faraway kingdom, in a town that sat by the sea . . .

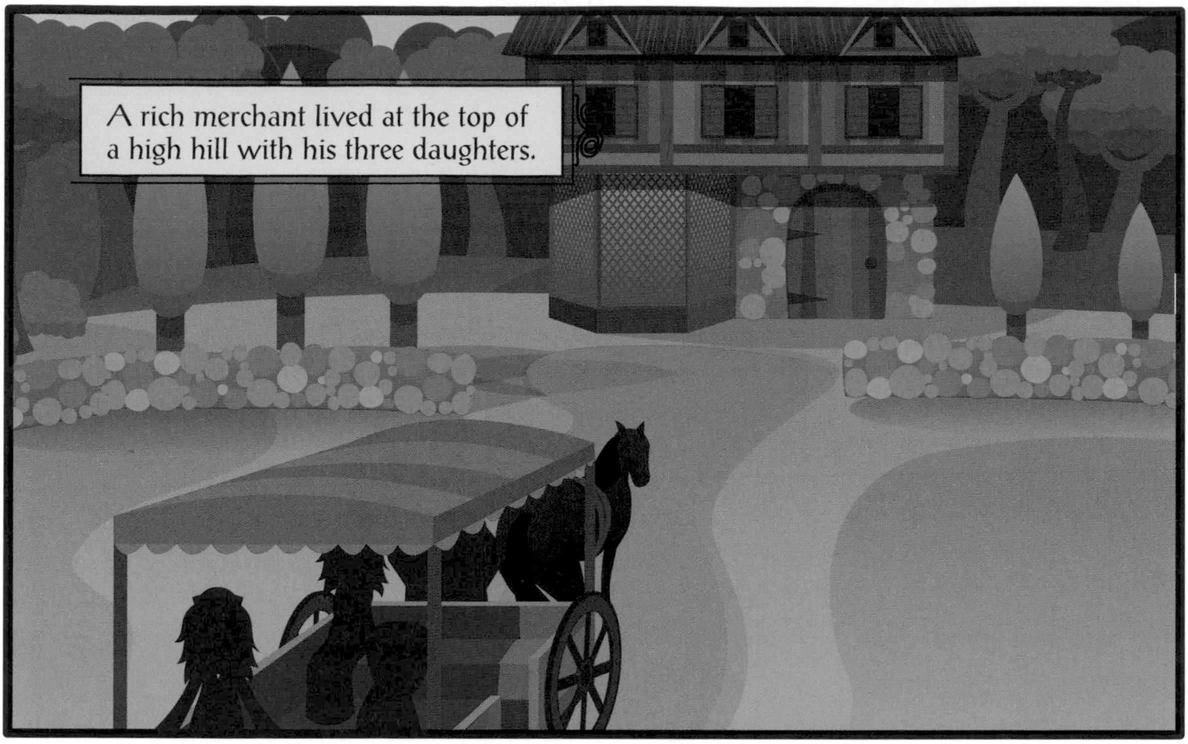
A rich merchant lived at the top of a high hill with his three daughters.

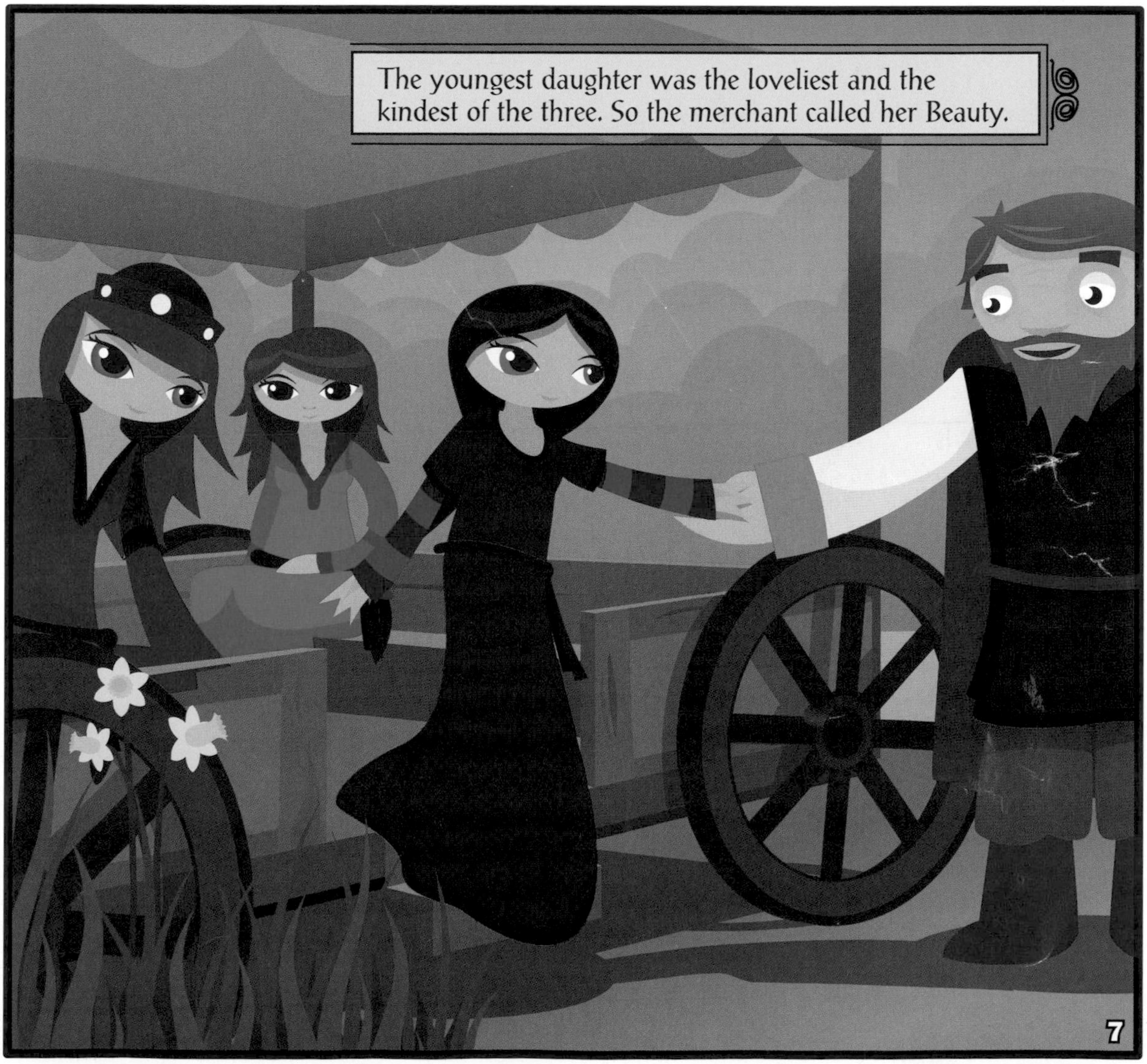
The youngest daughter was the loveliest and the kindest of the three. So the merchant called her Beauty.

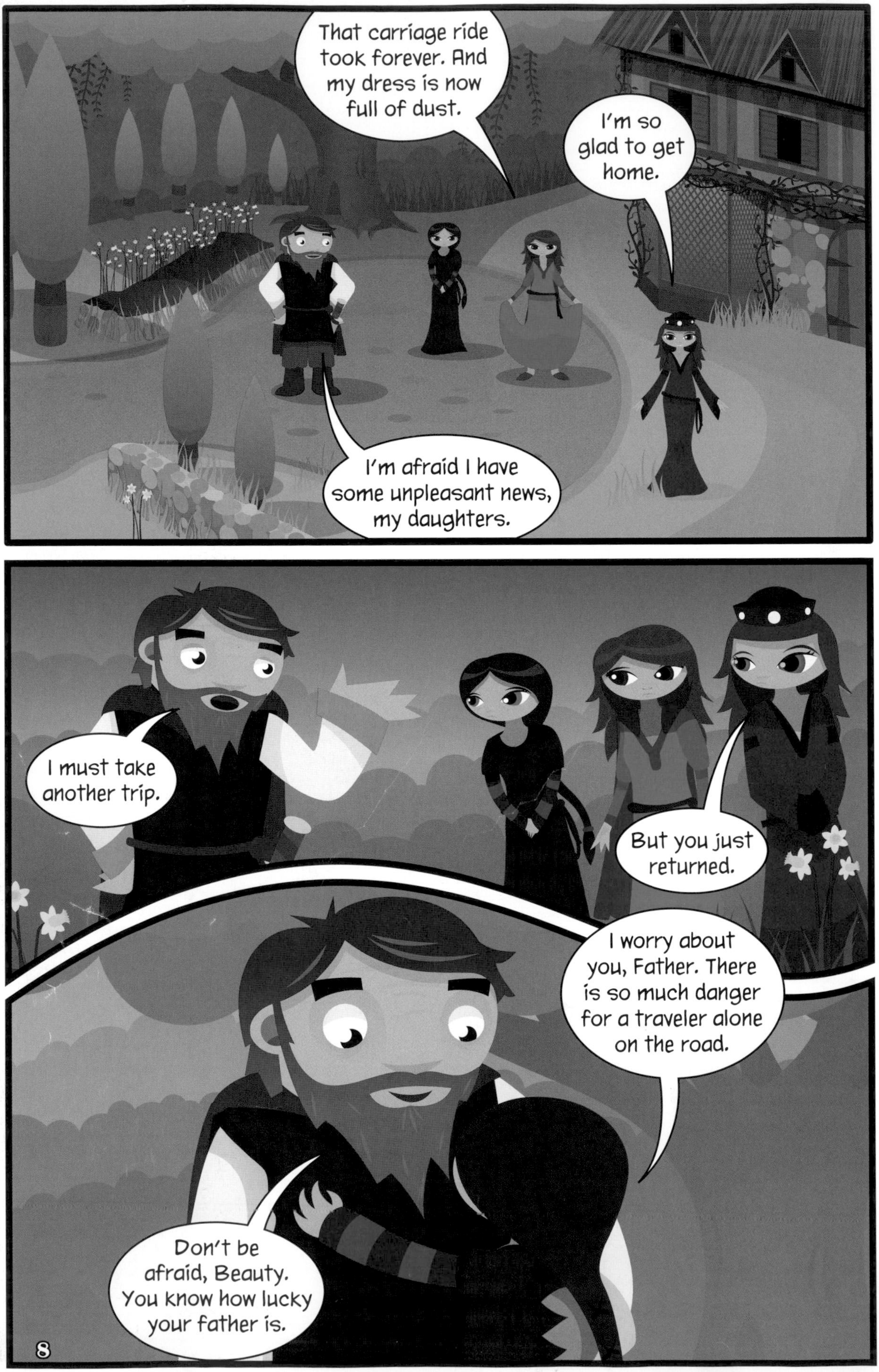
That carriage ride took forever. And my dress is now full of dust.
I'm so glad to get home.
I'm afraid I have some unpleasant news, my daughters.
I must take another trip.
But you just returned.
I worry about you, Father. There is so much danger for a traveler alone on the road.
Don't be afraid, Beauty. You know how lucky your father is.

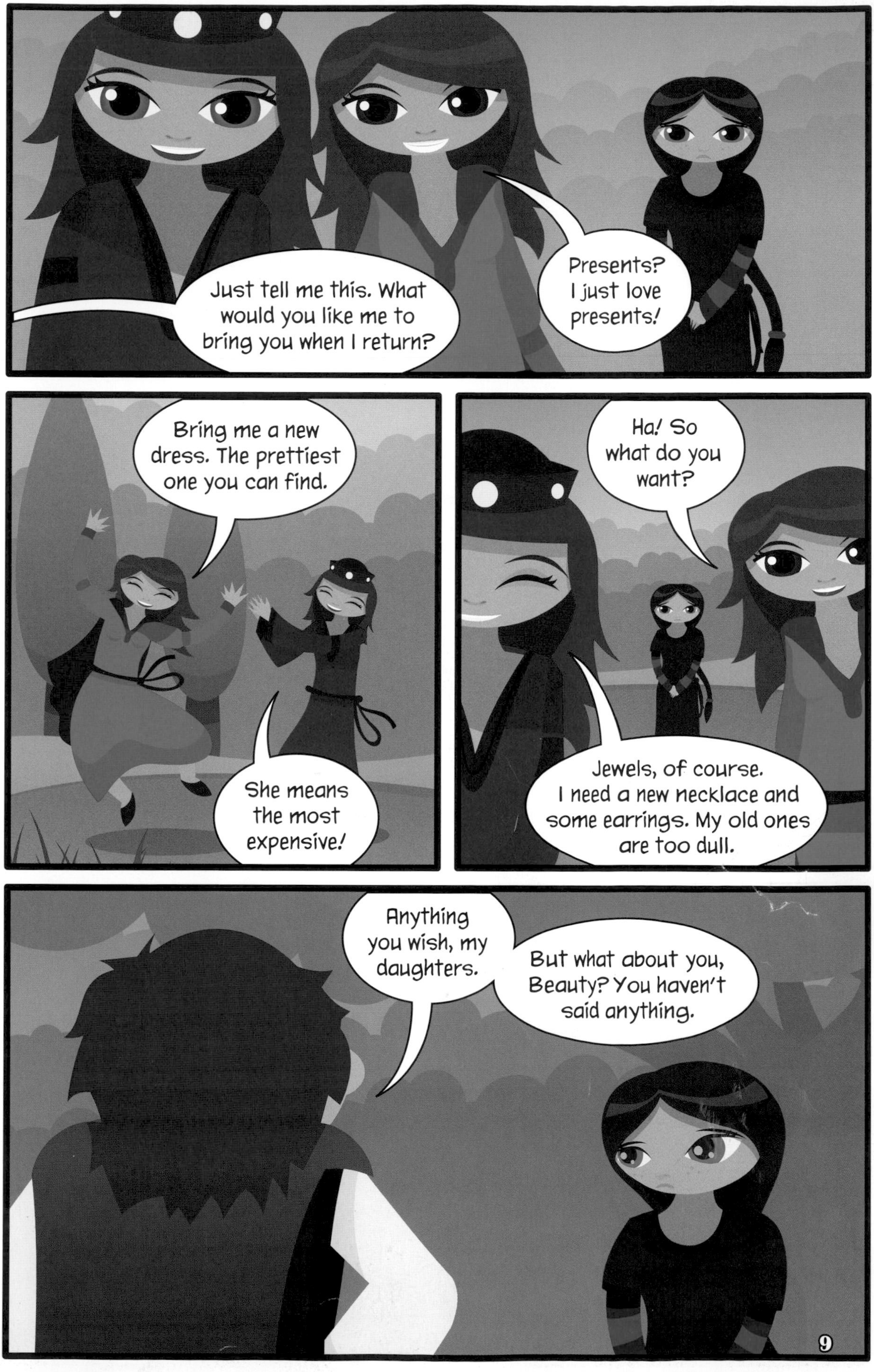
Just tell me this. What would you like me to bring you when I return?
Presents? I just love presents!
Bring me a new dress. The prettiest one you can find.
She means the most expensive!
Ha! So what do you want?
Jewels, of course. I need a new necklace and some earrings. My old ones are too dull.
Anything you wish, my daughters.
But what about you, Beauty? You haven't said anything.

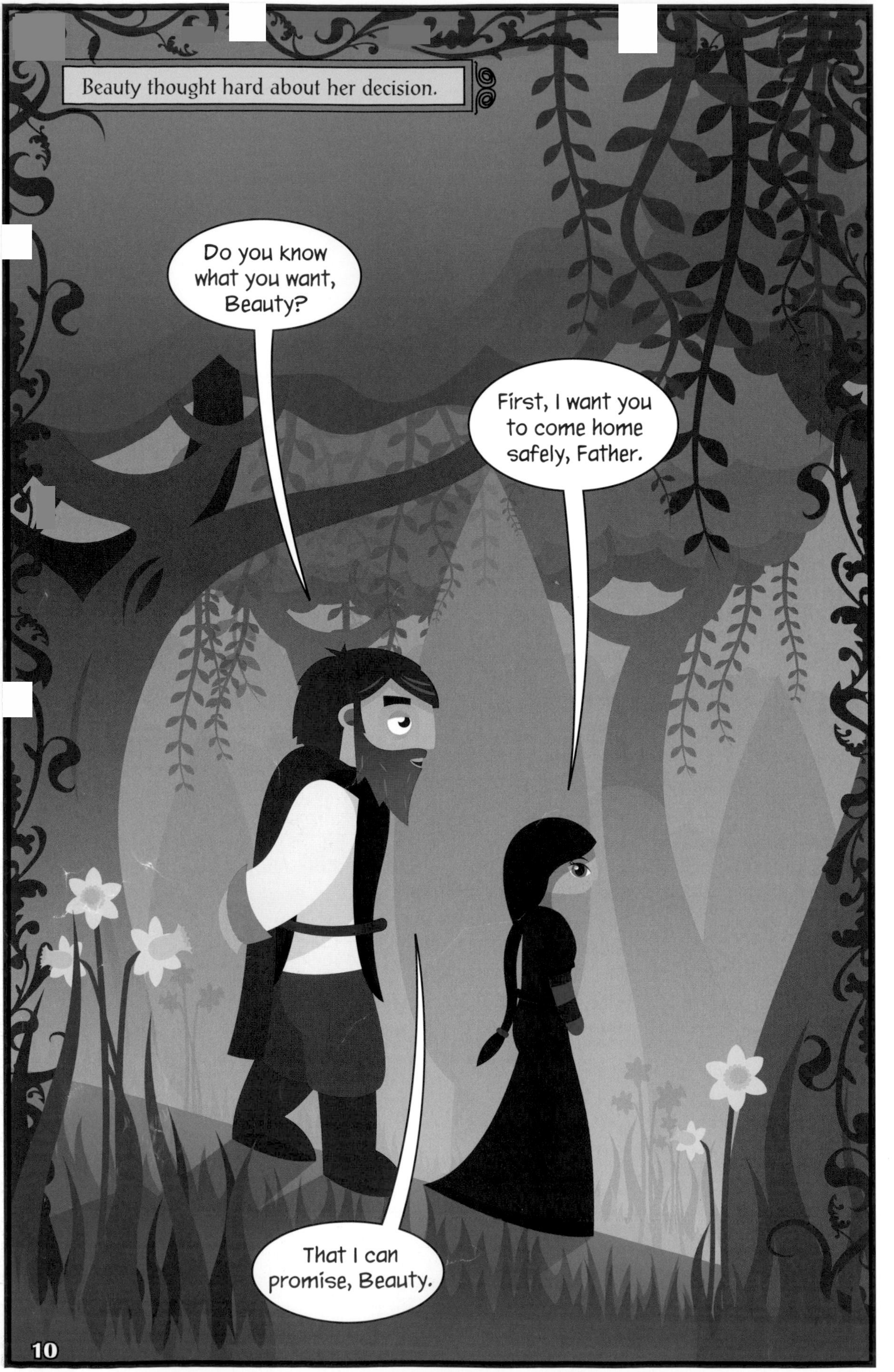
Beauty thought hard about her decision.
Do you know what you want, Beauty?
First, I want you to come home safely, Father.
That I can promise, Beauty.

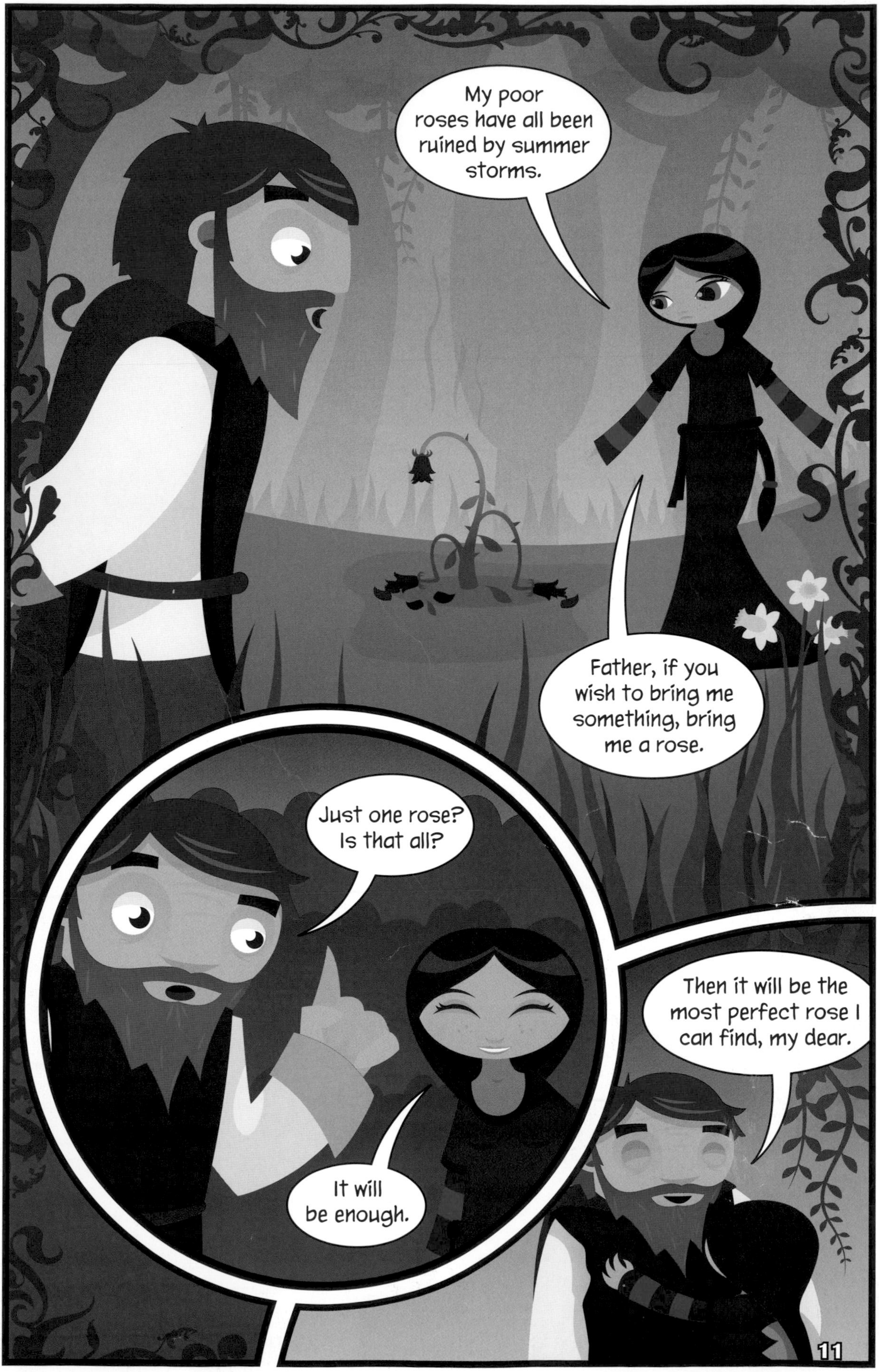
My poor roses have all been ruined by summer storms.
Father, if you wish to bring me something, bring me a rose.
Just one rose? Is that all?
It will be enough.
Then it will be the most perfect rose I can find, my dear.

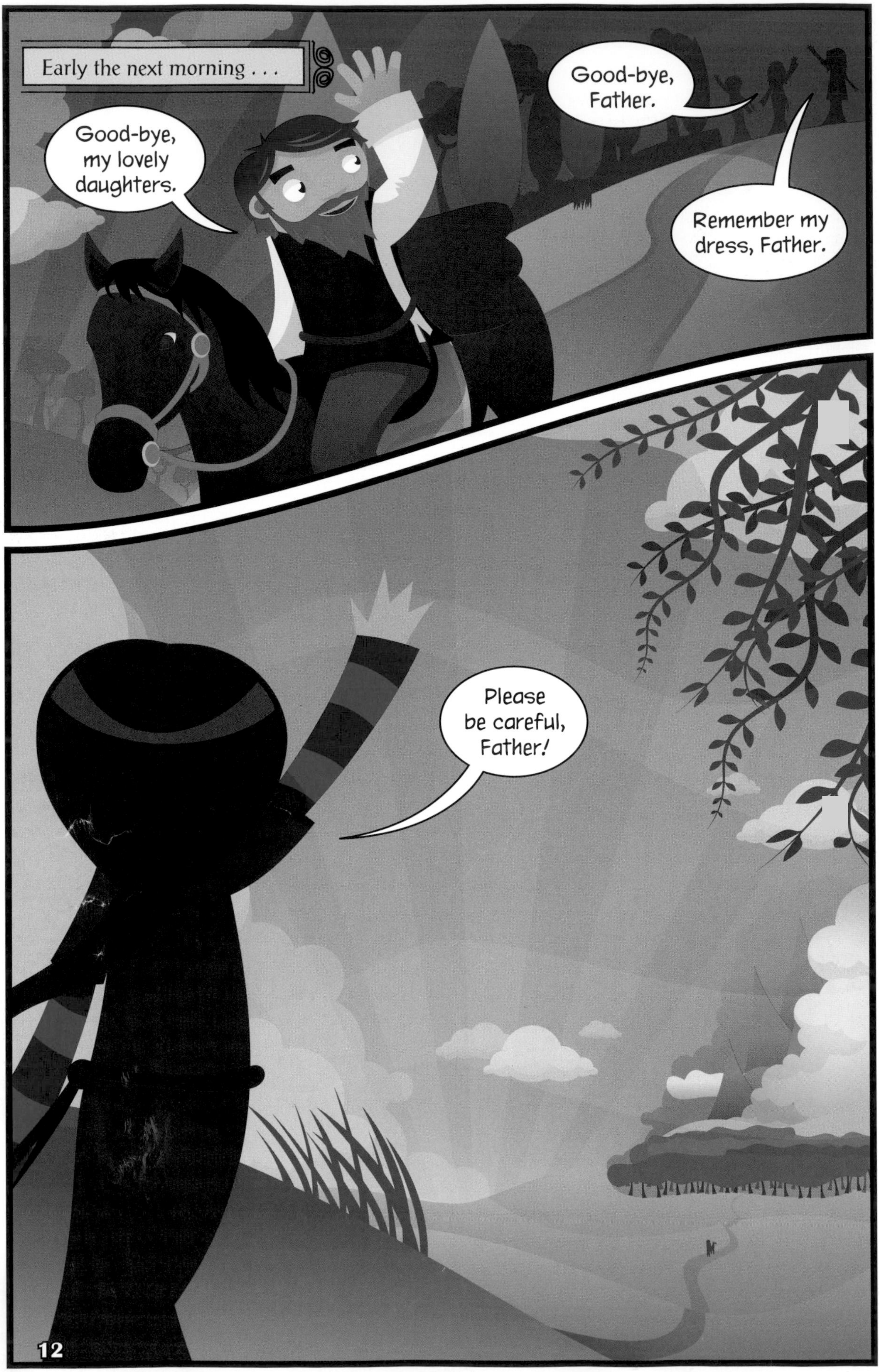
Early the next morning . . .
Good-bye, my lovely daughters.
Good-bye, Father.
Remember my dress, Father.
Please be careful, Father!

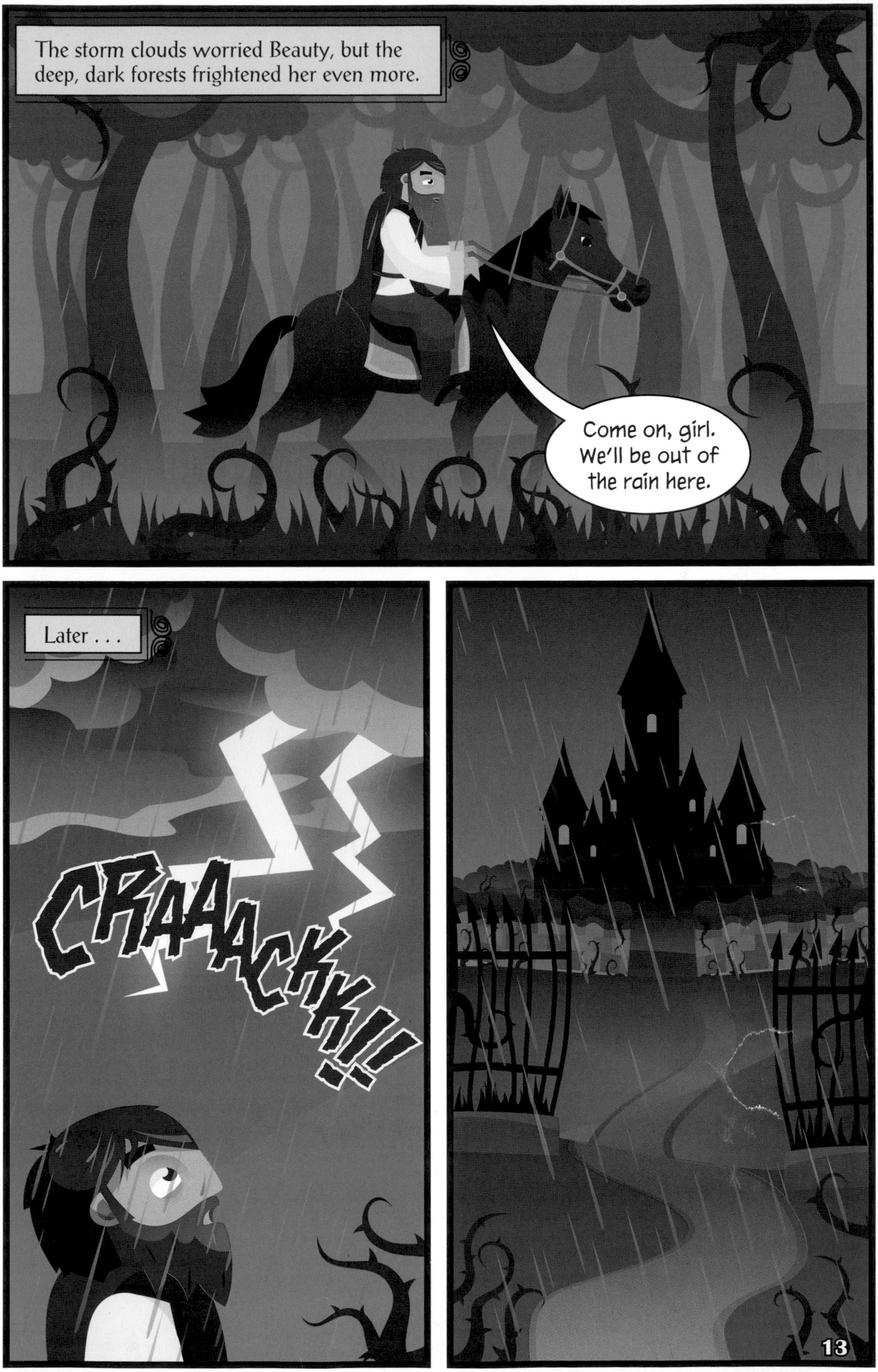
The storm clouds worried Beauty, but the deep, dark forests frightened her even more.
Come on, girl. We'll be out of the rain here.
Later . . .
CRAAACKK!!!

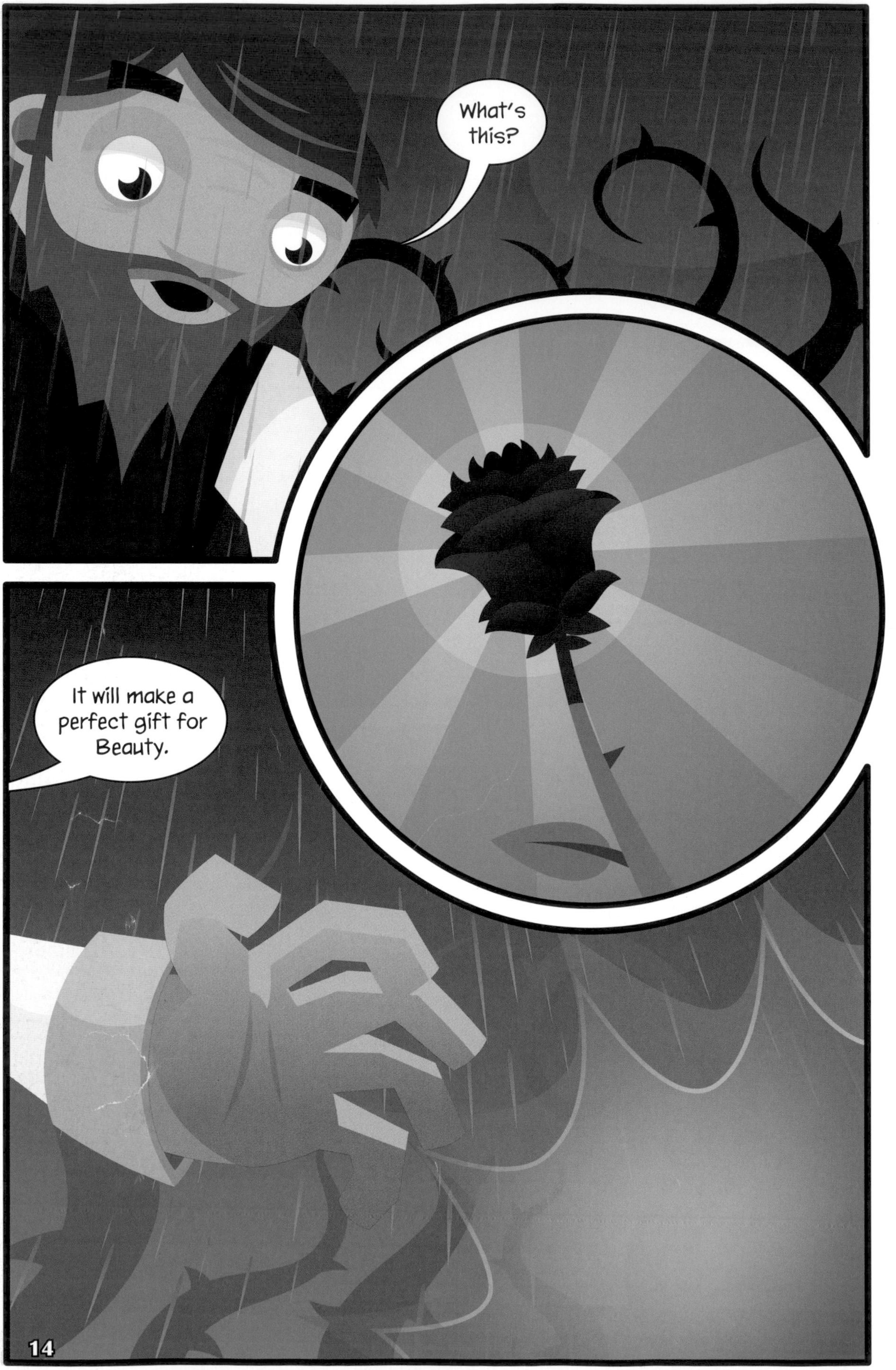
What's this?
It will make a perfect gift for Beauty.

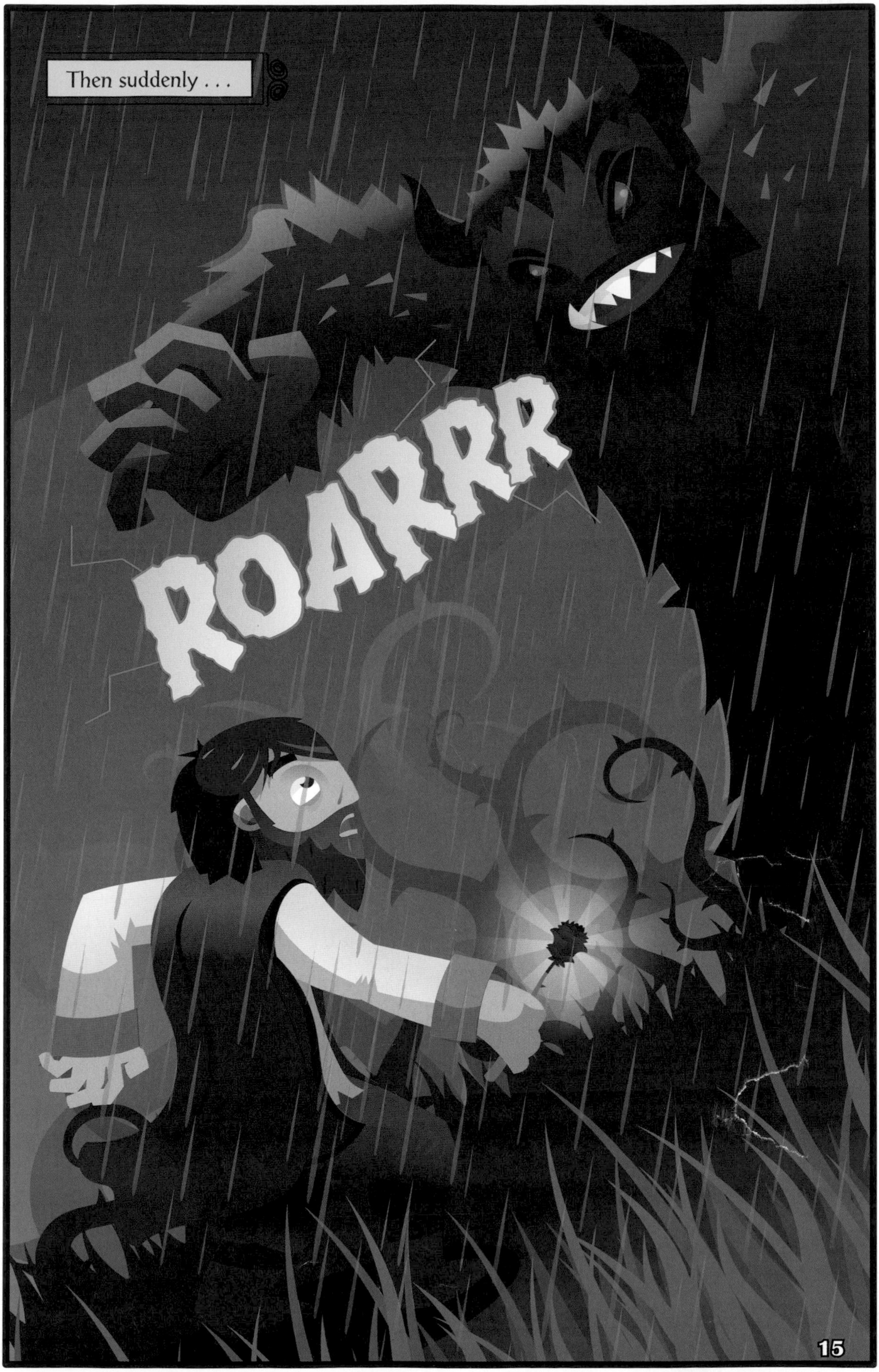
Then suddenly . . .
ROARRR

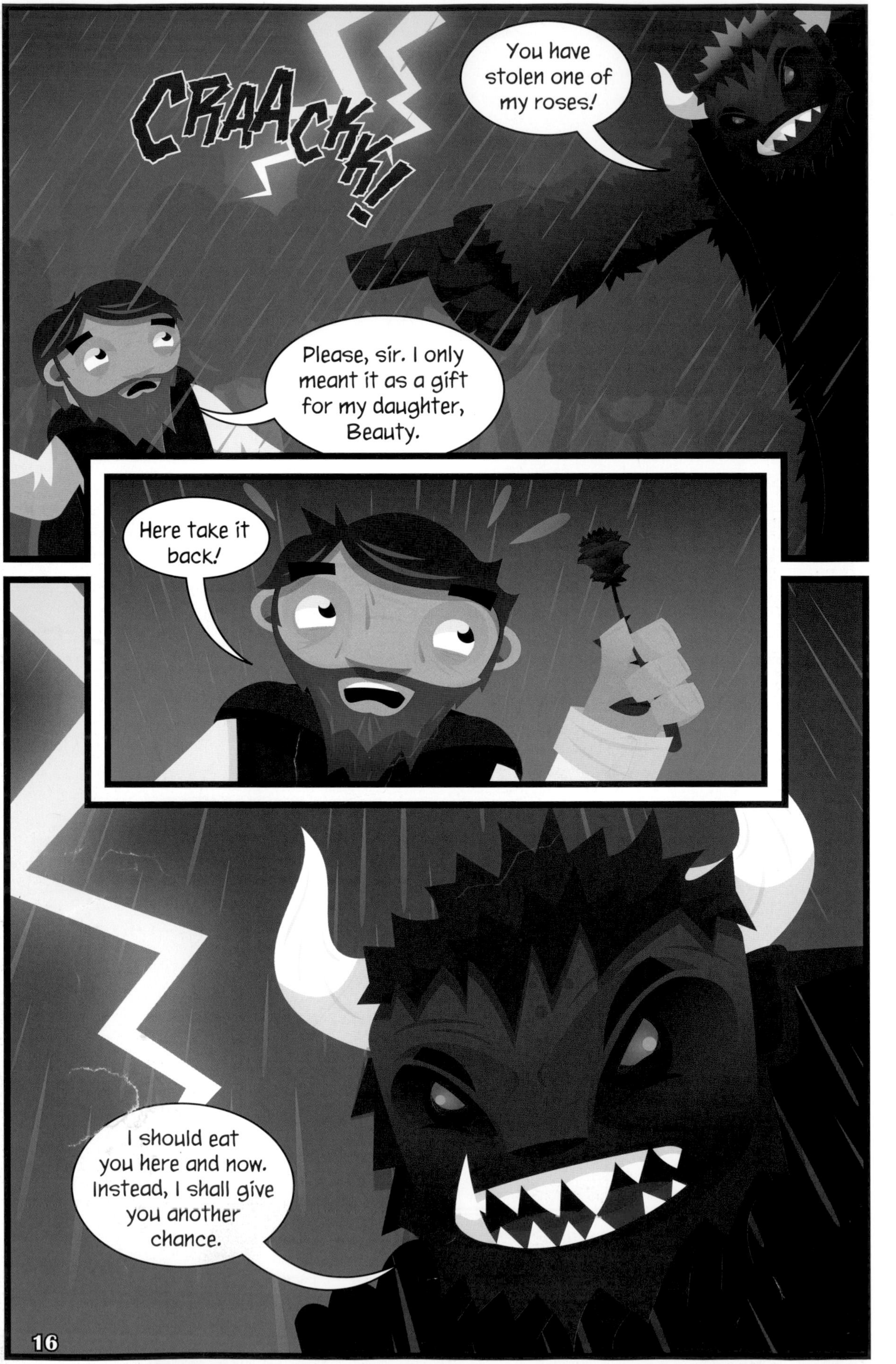
CRAACKK!
You have stolen one of my roses!
Please, sir. I only meant it as a gift for my daughter, Beauty.
Here take it back!
I should eat you here and now. Instead, I shall give you another chance.

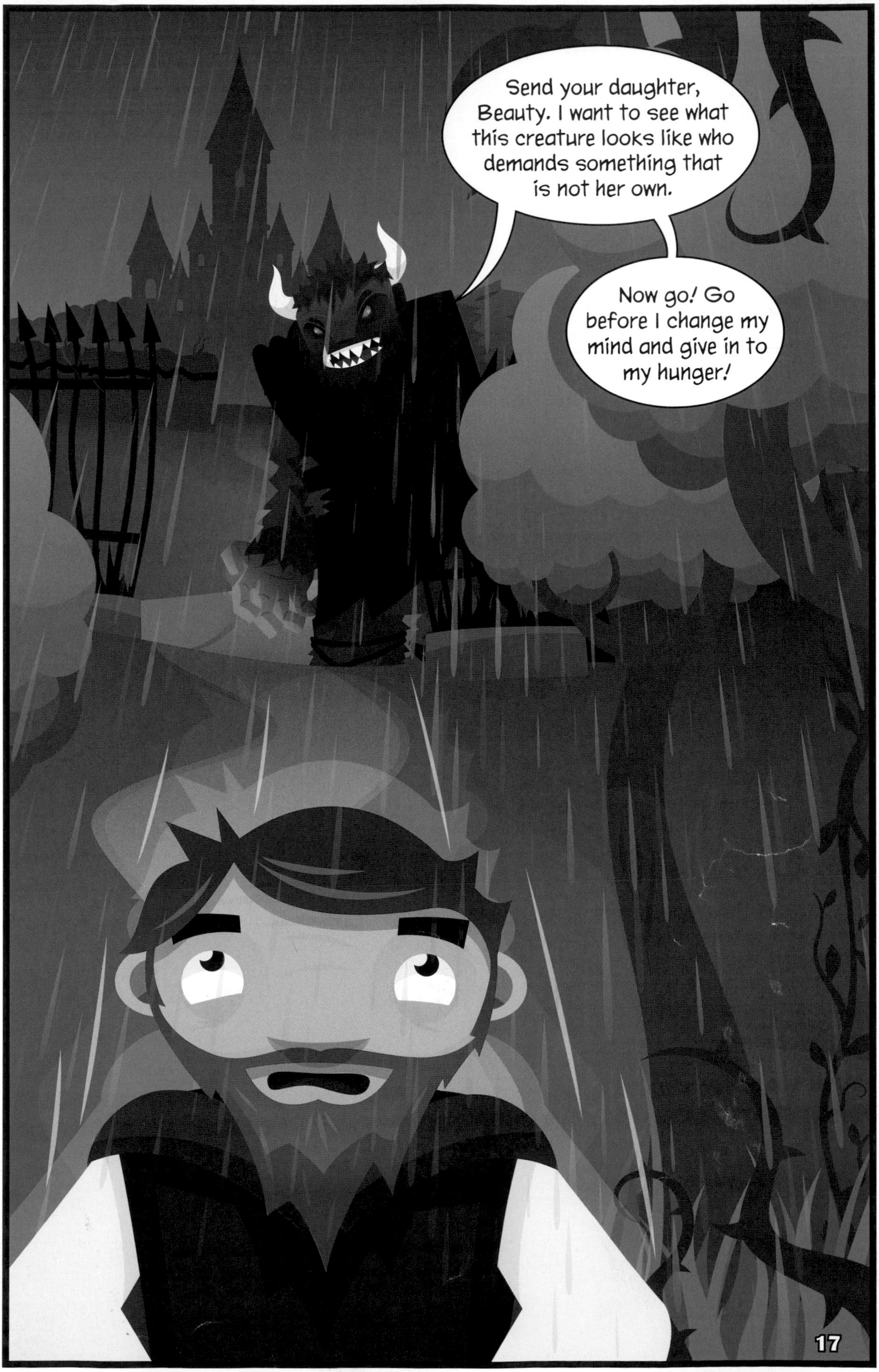
Send your daughter, Beauty. I want to see what this creature looks like who demands something that is not her own.
Now go! Go before I change my mind and give in to my hunger!

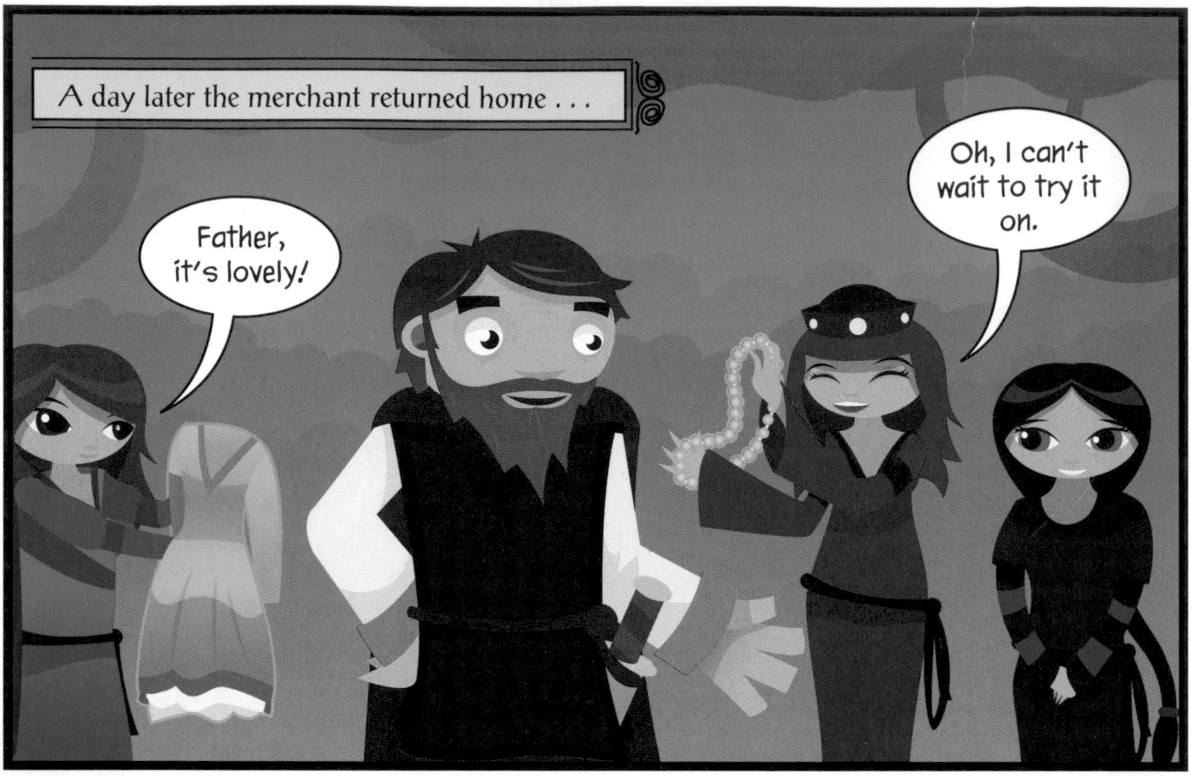
A day later the merchant returned home . . .
Father, it's lovely!
Oh, I can't wait to try it on.

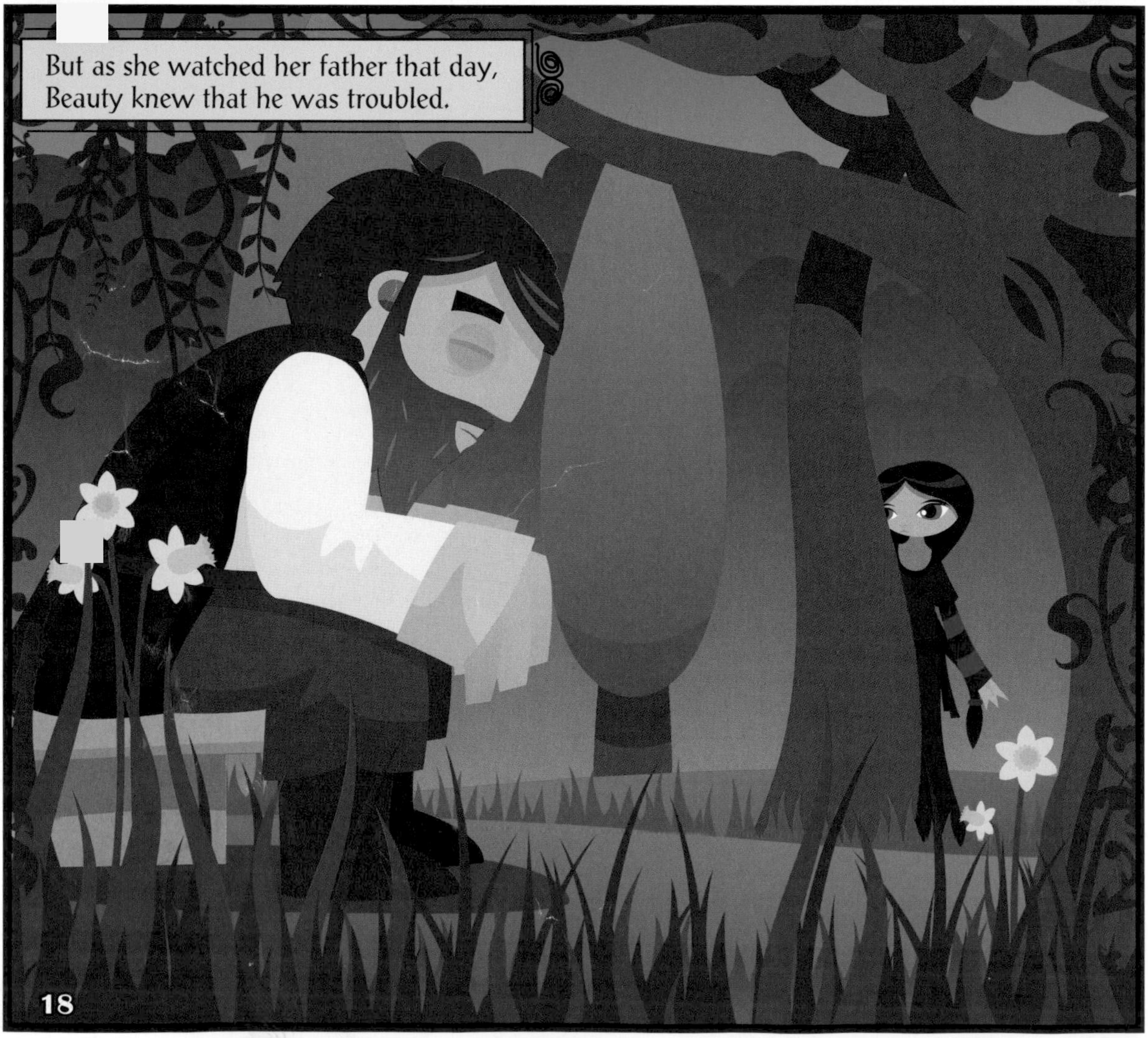
But as she watched her father that day, Beauty knew that he was troubled.

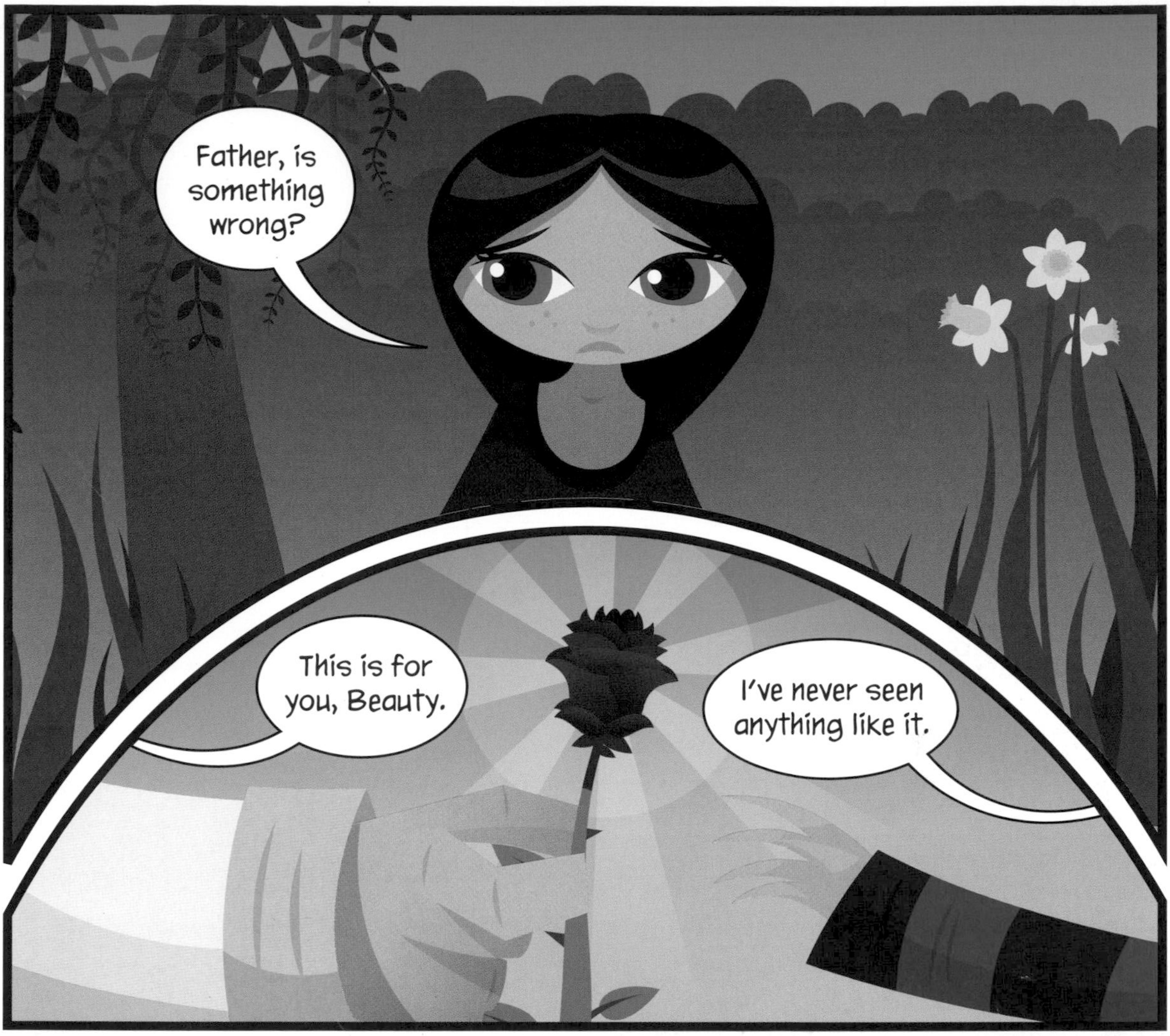
Father, is something wrong?
This is for you, Beauty.
I've never seen anything like it.

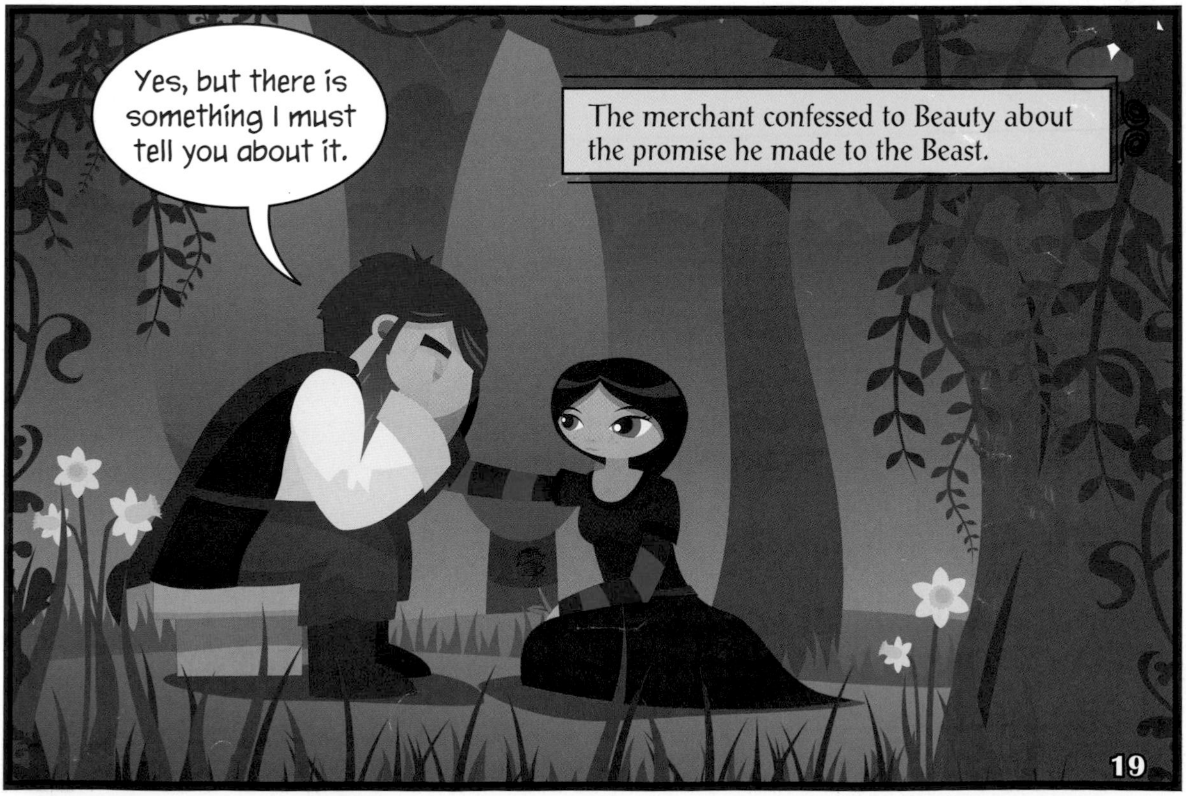
Yes, but there is something I must tell you about it.
The merchant confessed to Beauty about the promise he made to the Beast.

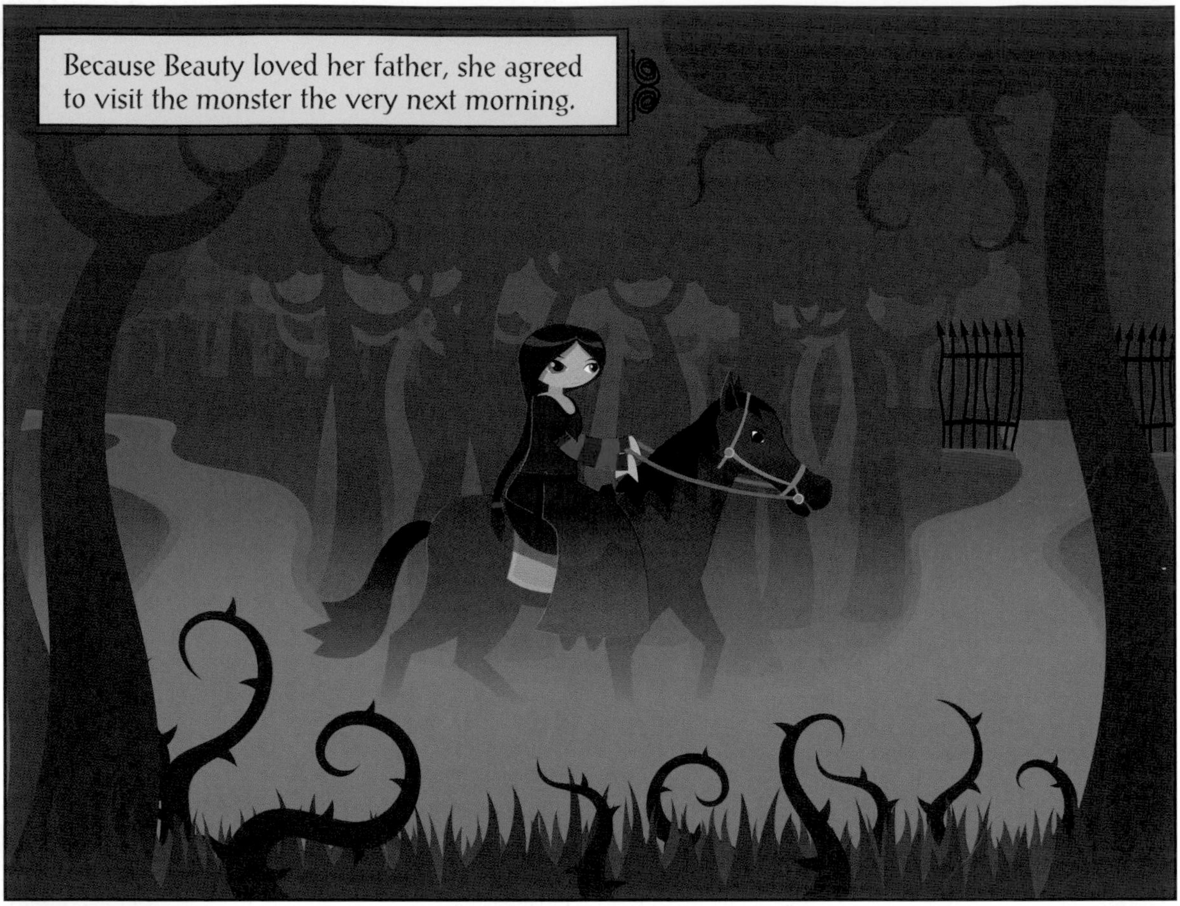
Because Beauty loved her father, she agreed to visit the monster the very next morning.

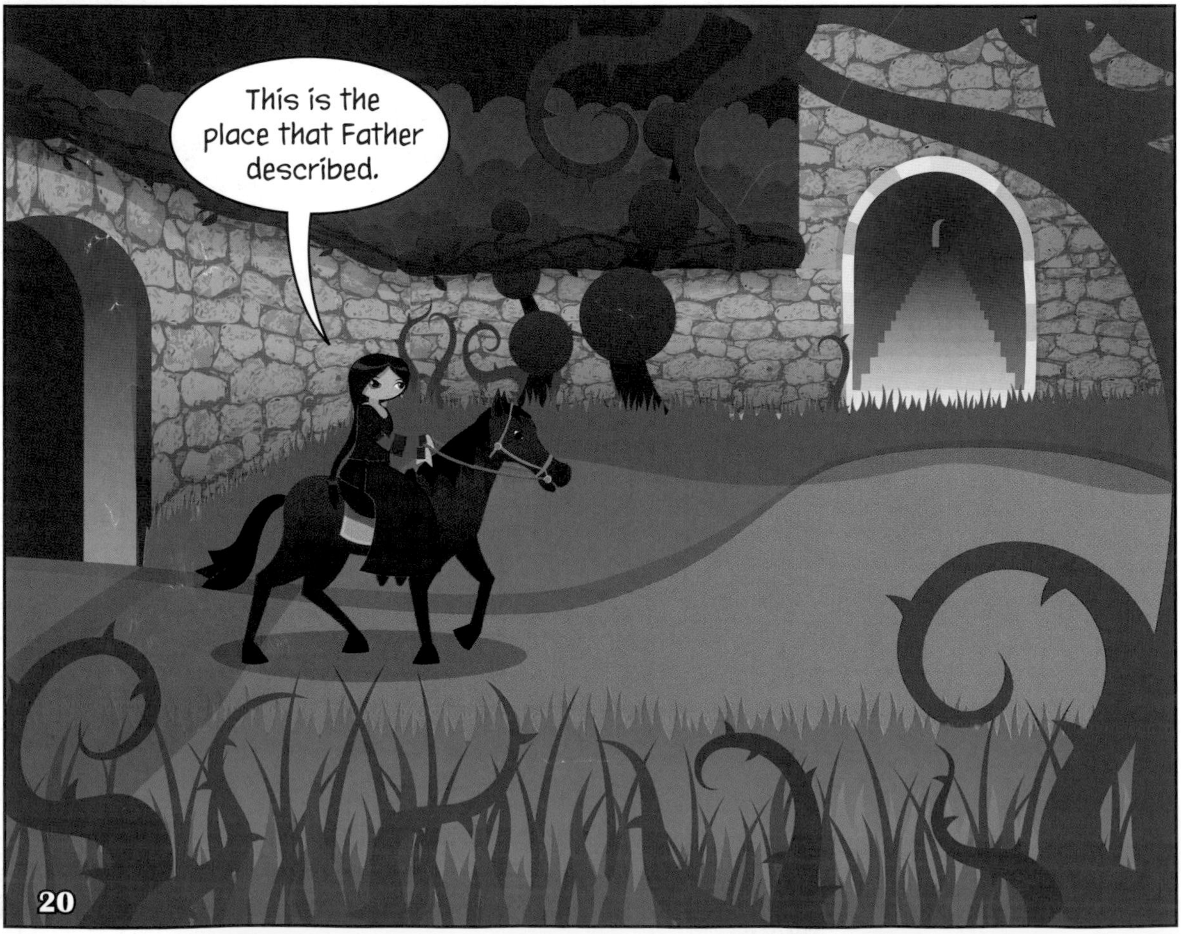
This is the place that Father described.

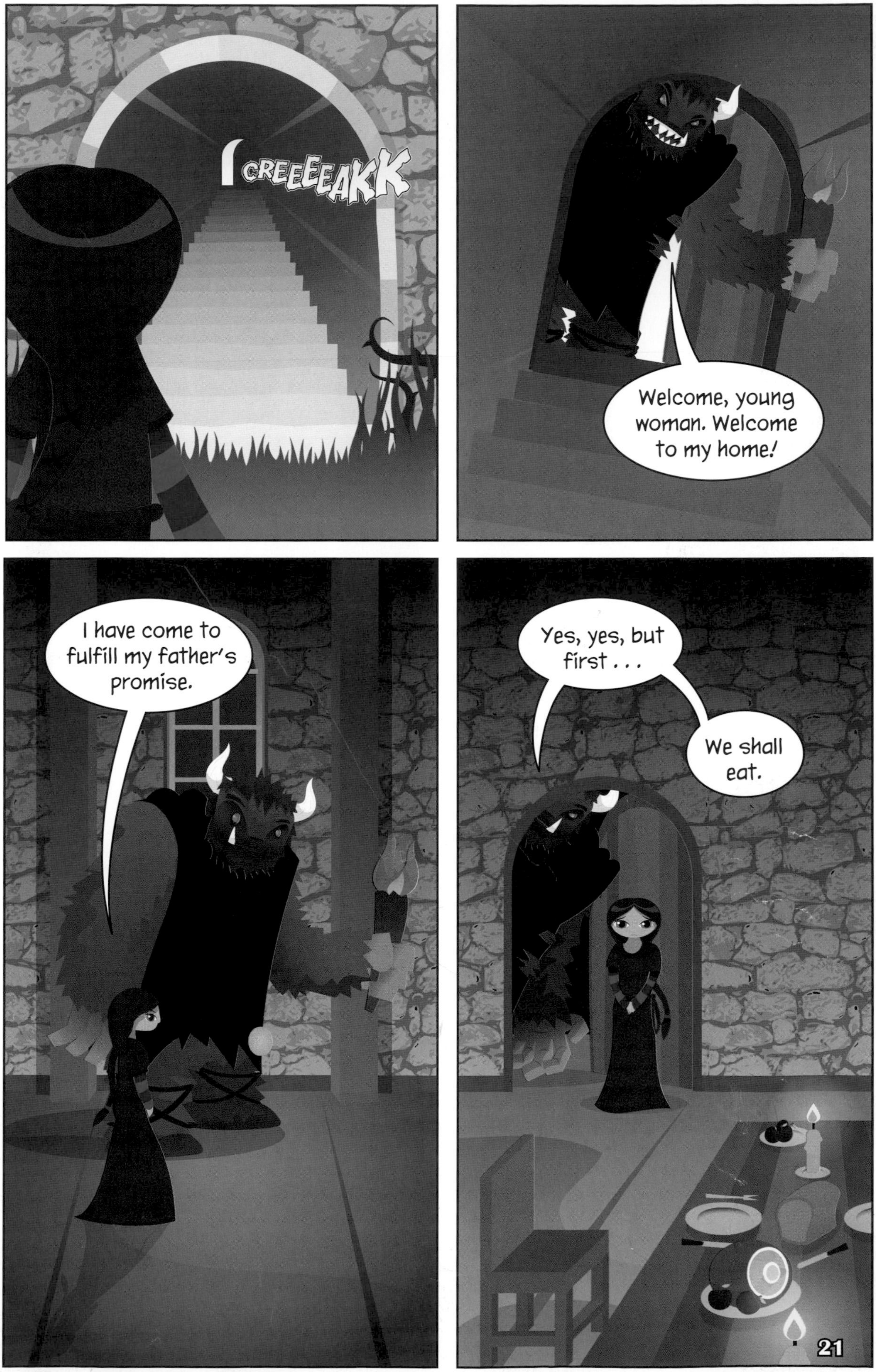
CREEEEAKK
Welcome, young woman. Welcome to my home!
I have come to fulfill my father's promise.
Yes, yes, but first . . .
We shall eat.

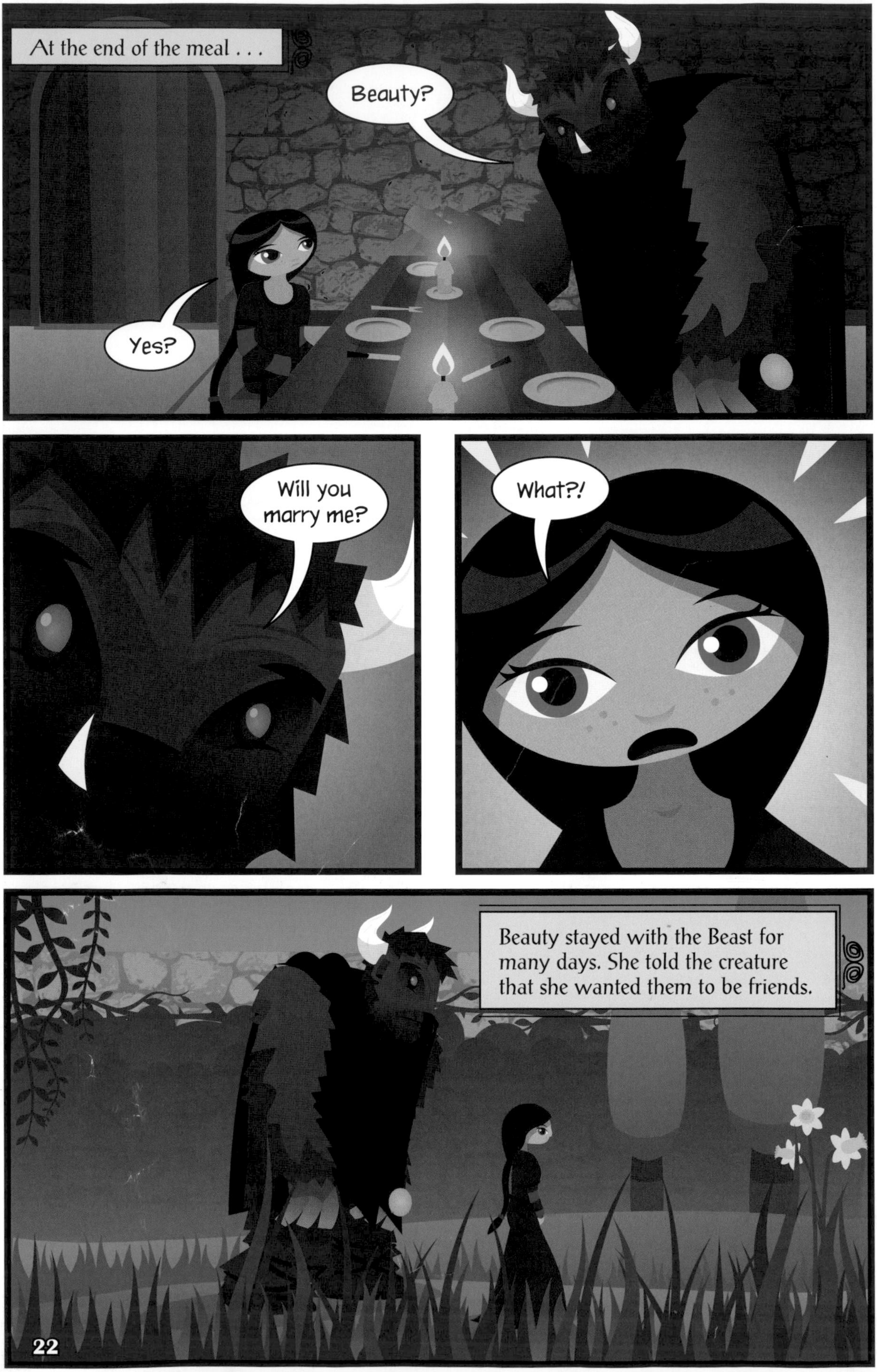
At the end of the meal . . .
Beauty?
Yes?
Will you marry me?
What?!
Beauty stayed with the Beast for many days. She told the creature that she wanted them to be friends.

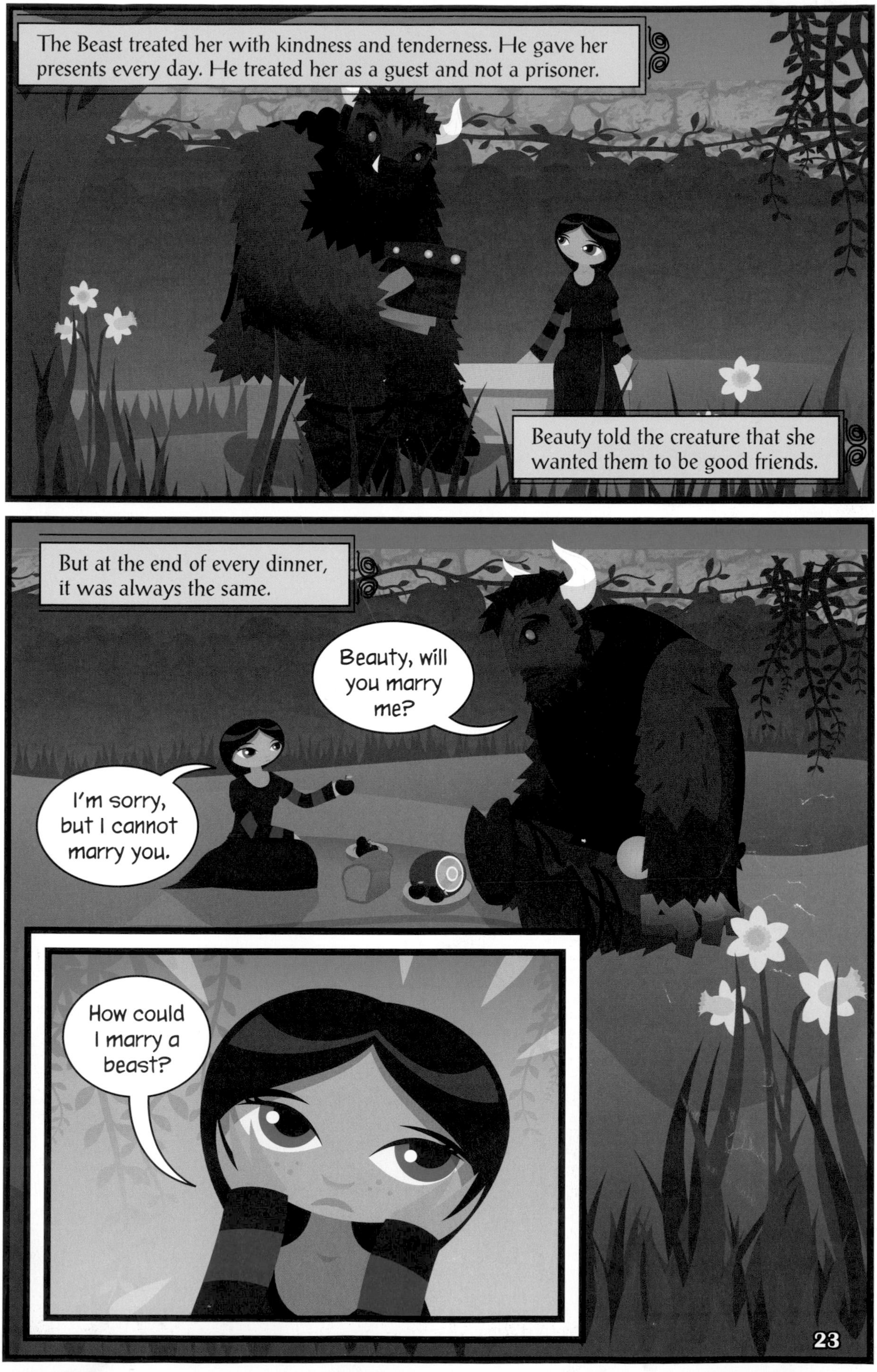
The Beast treated her with kindness and tenderness. He gave her presents every day. He treated her as a guest and not a prisoner.
Beauty told the creature that she wanted them to be good friends.
But at the end of every dinner, it was always the same.
Beauty, will you marry me?
I'm sorry, but I cannot marry you.
How could I marry a beast?

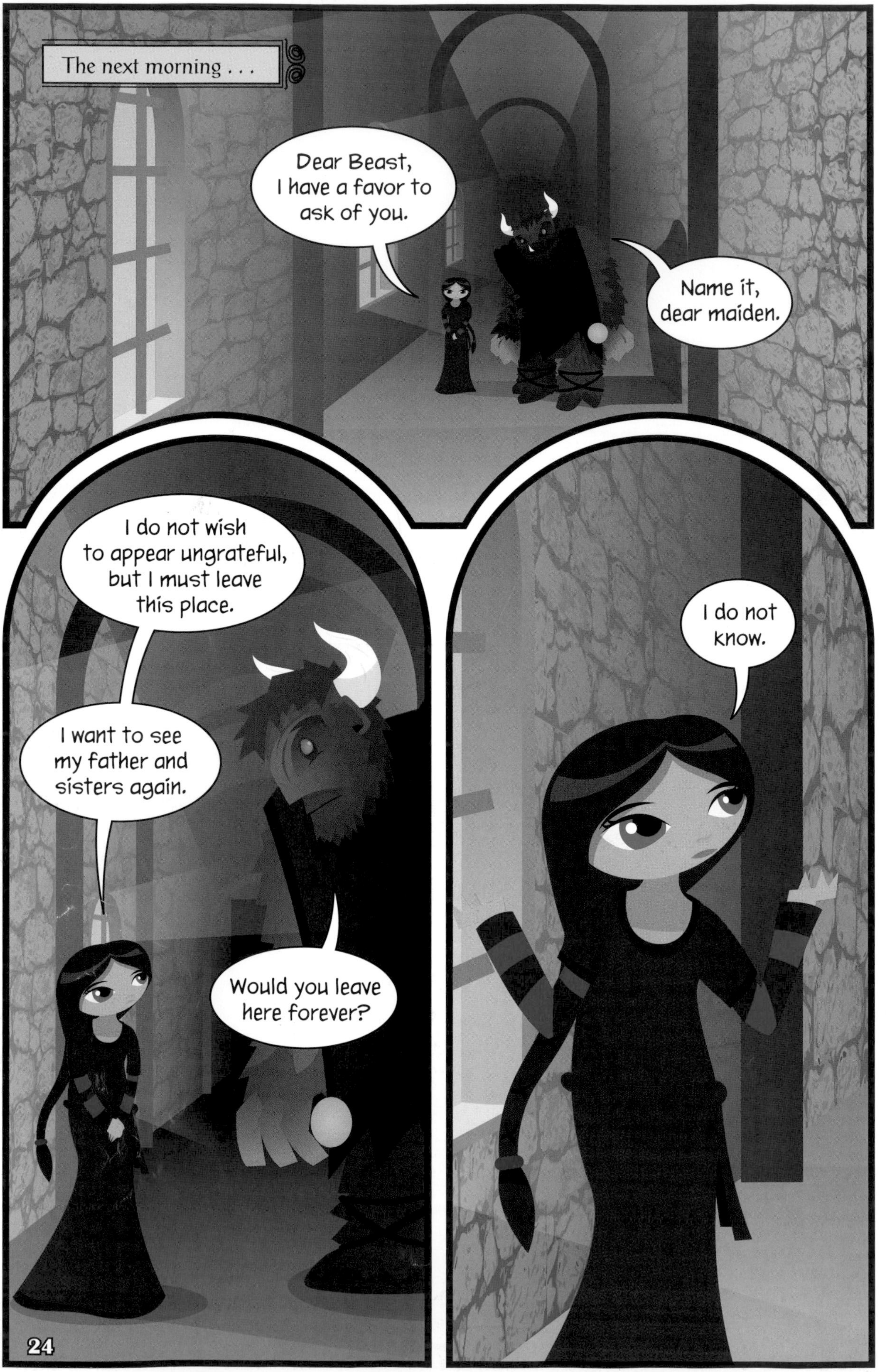
The next morning . . .
Dear Beast, I have a favor to ask of you.
Name it, dear maiden.
I do not wish to appear ungrateful, but I must leave this place.
I want to see my father and sisters again.
Would you leave here forever?
I do not know.

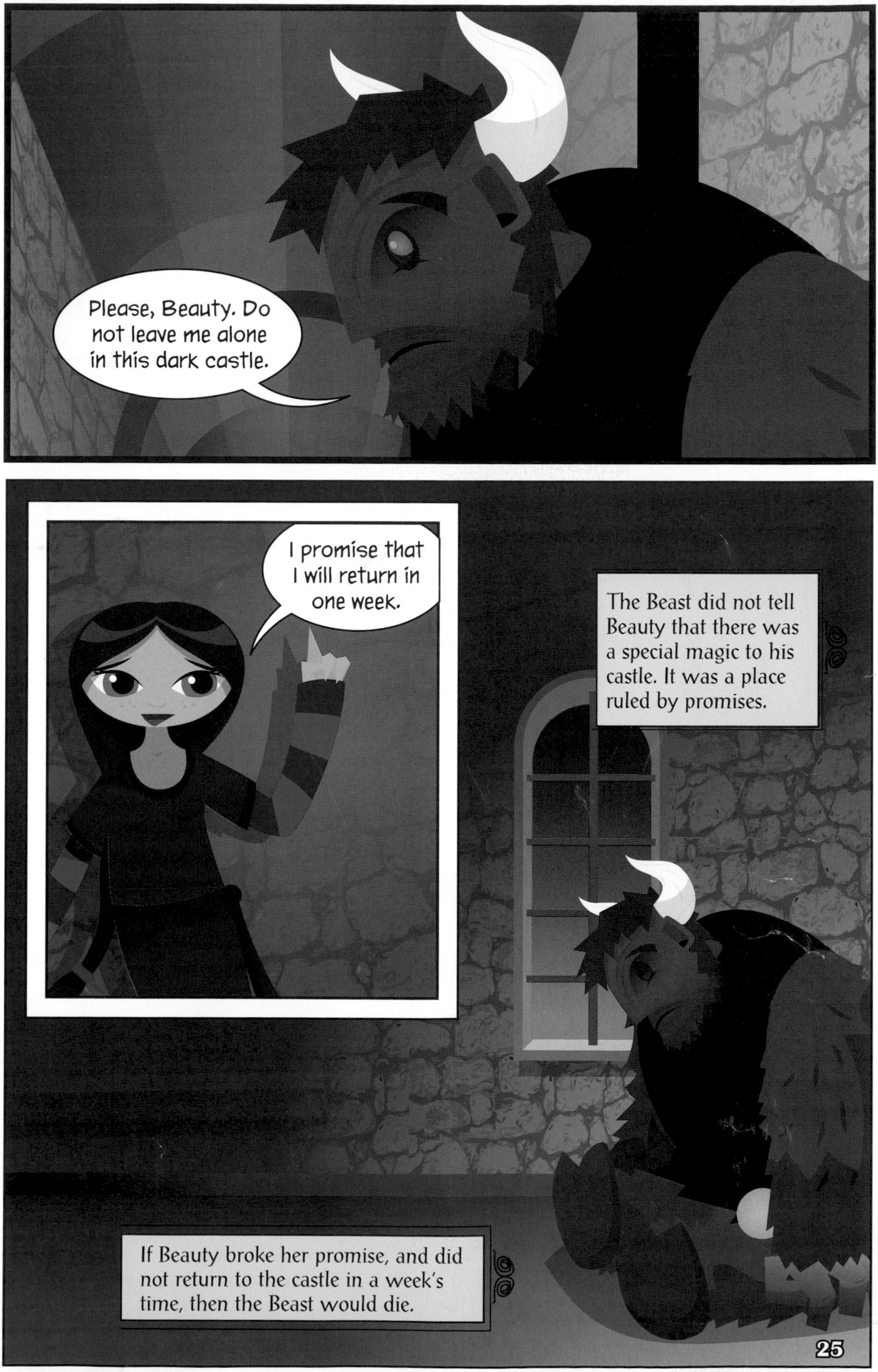
Please, Beauty. Do not leave me alone in this dark castle.
I promise that I will return in one week.
The Beast did not tell Beauty that there was a special magic to his castle. It was a place ruled by promises.
If Beauty broke her promise, and did not return to the castle in a week's time, then the Beast would die.

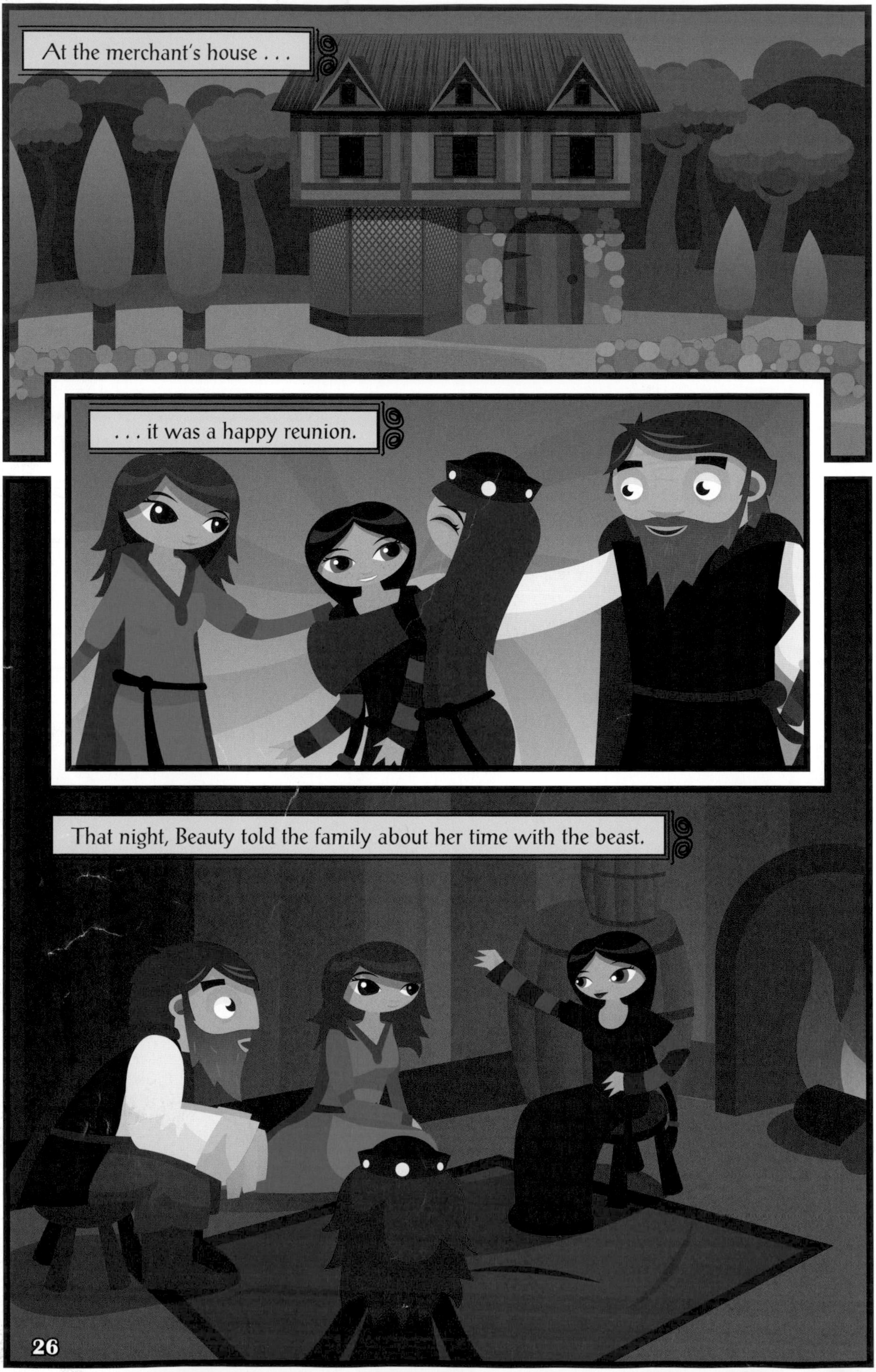
At the merchant's house . . .
. . . it was a happy reunion.
That night, Beauty told the family about her time with the beast.

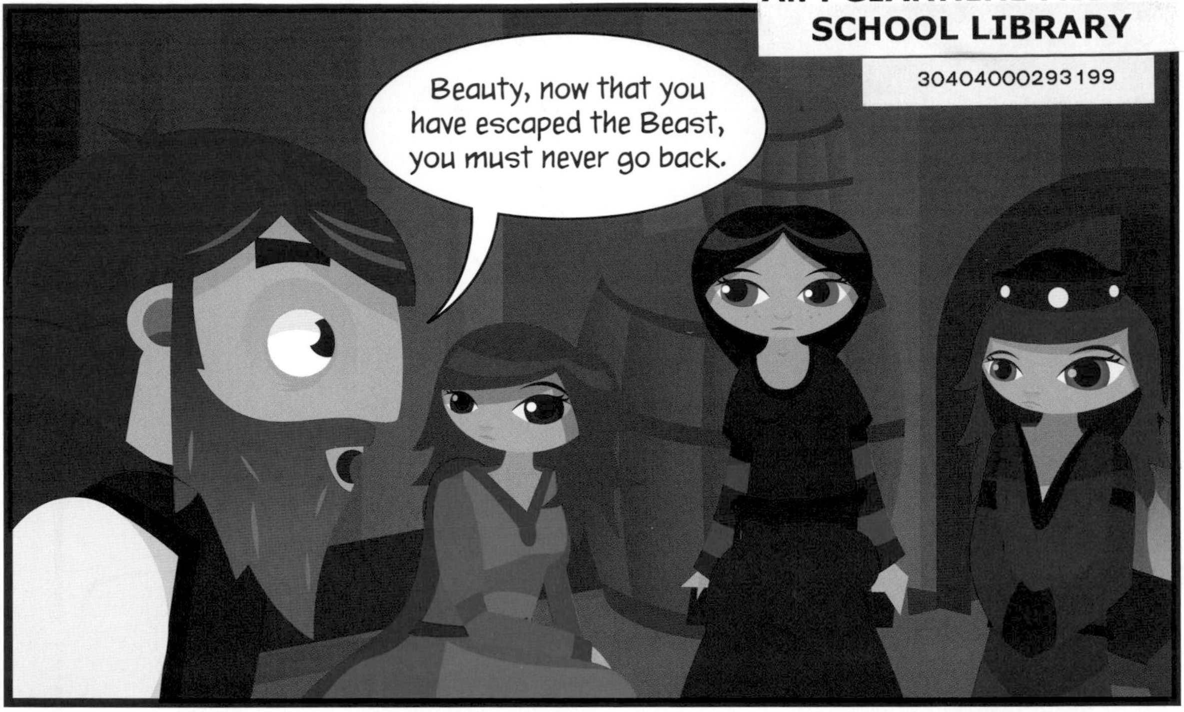
Beauty, now that you have escaped the Beast, you must never go back.

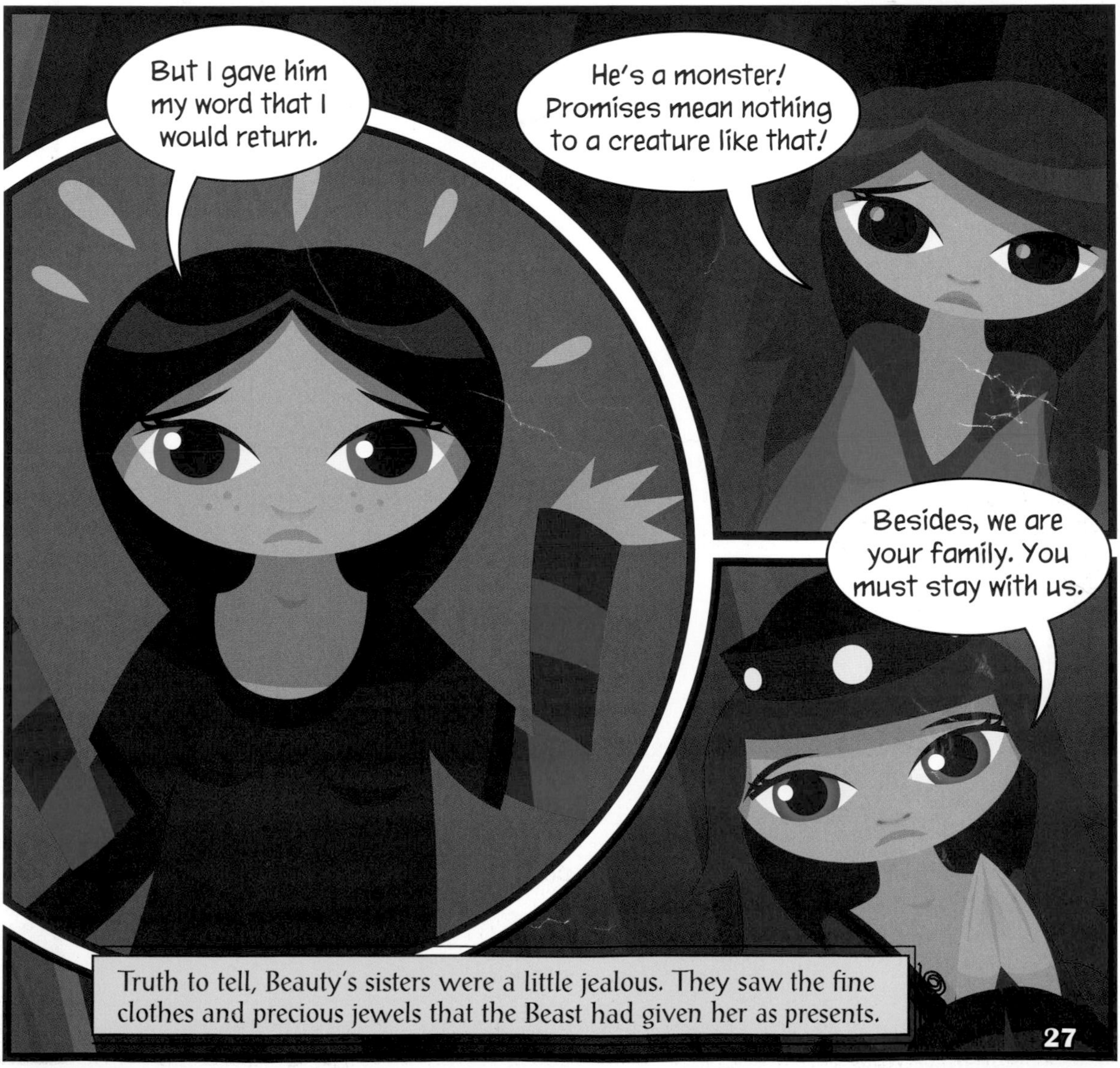
But I gave him my word that I would return.
He's a monster! Promises mean nothing to a creature like that!
Besides, we are your family. You must stay with us.
Truth to tell, Beauty's sisters were a little jealous. They saw the fine clothes and precious jewels that the Beast had given her as presents.

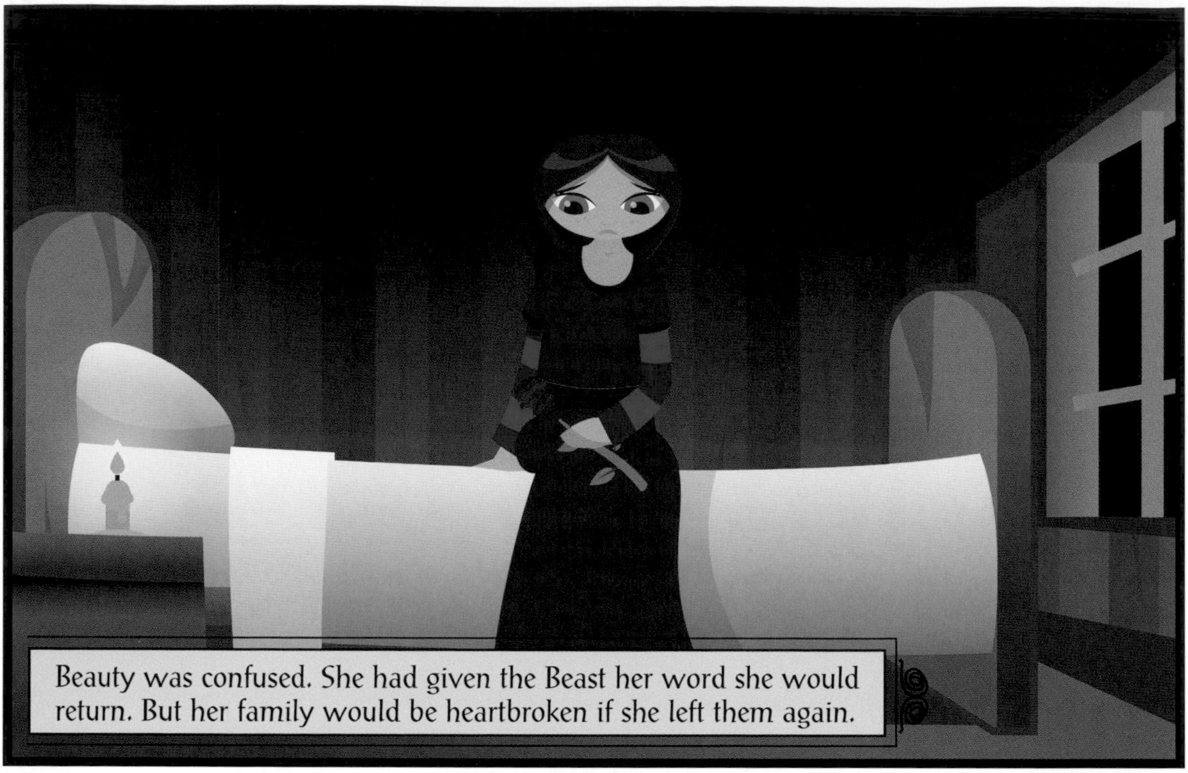
Beauty was confused. She had given the Beast her word she would return. But her family would be heartbroken if she left them again.

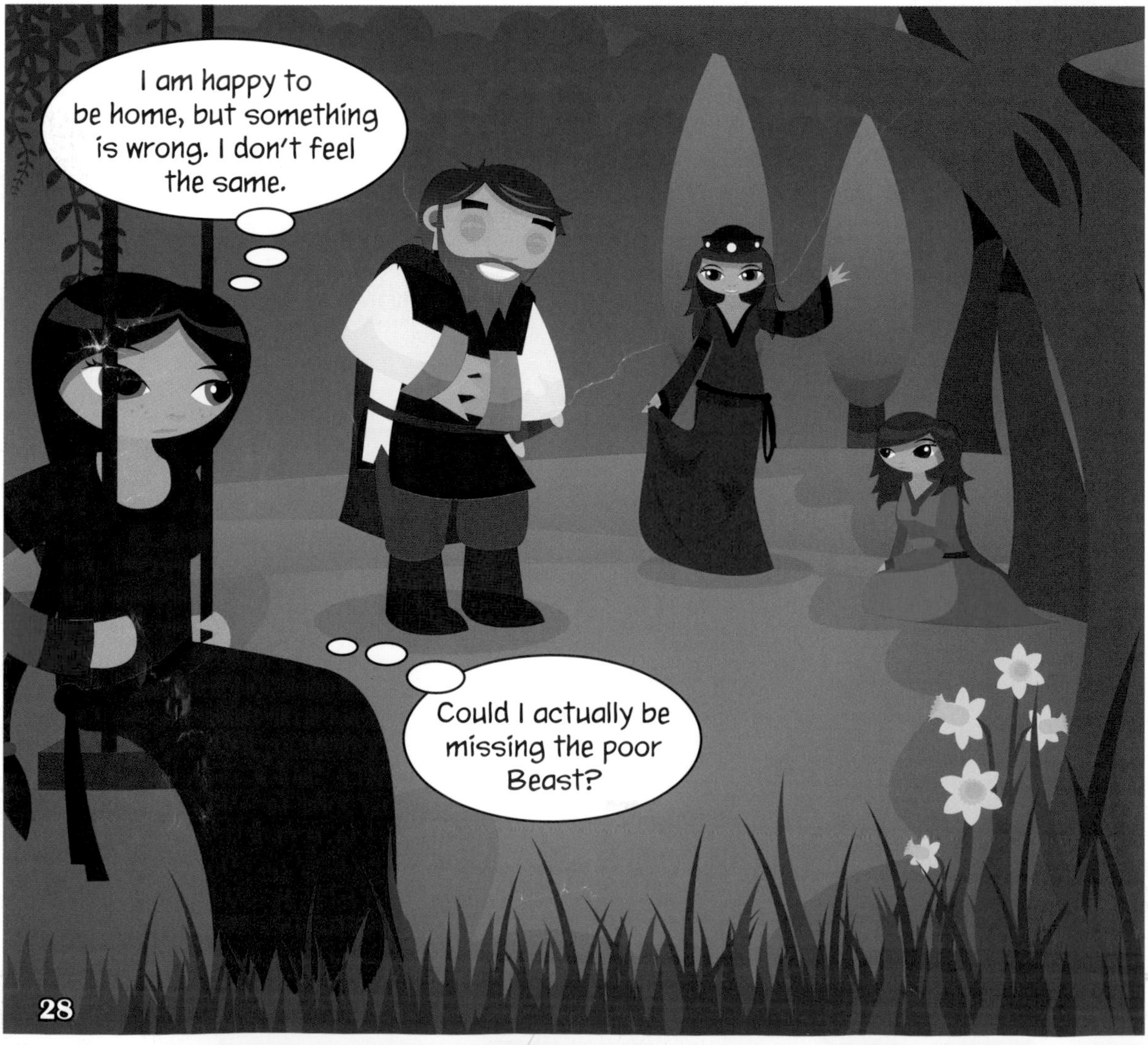
I am happy to be home, but something is wrong. I don't feel the same.
Could I actually be missing the poor Beast?

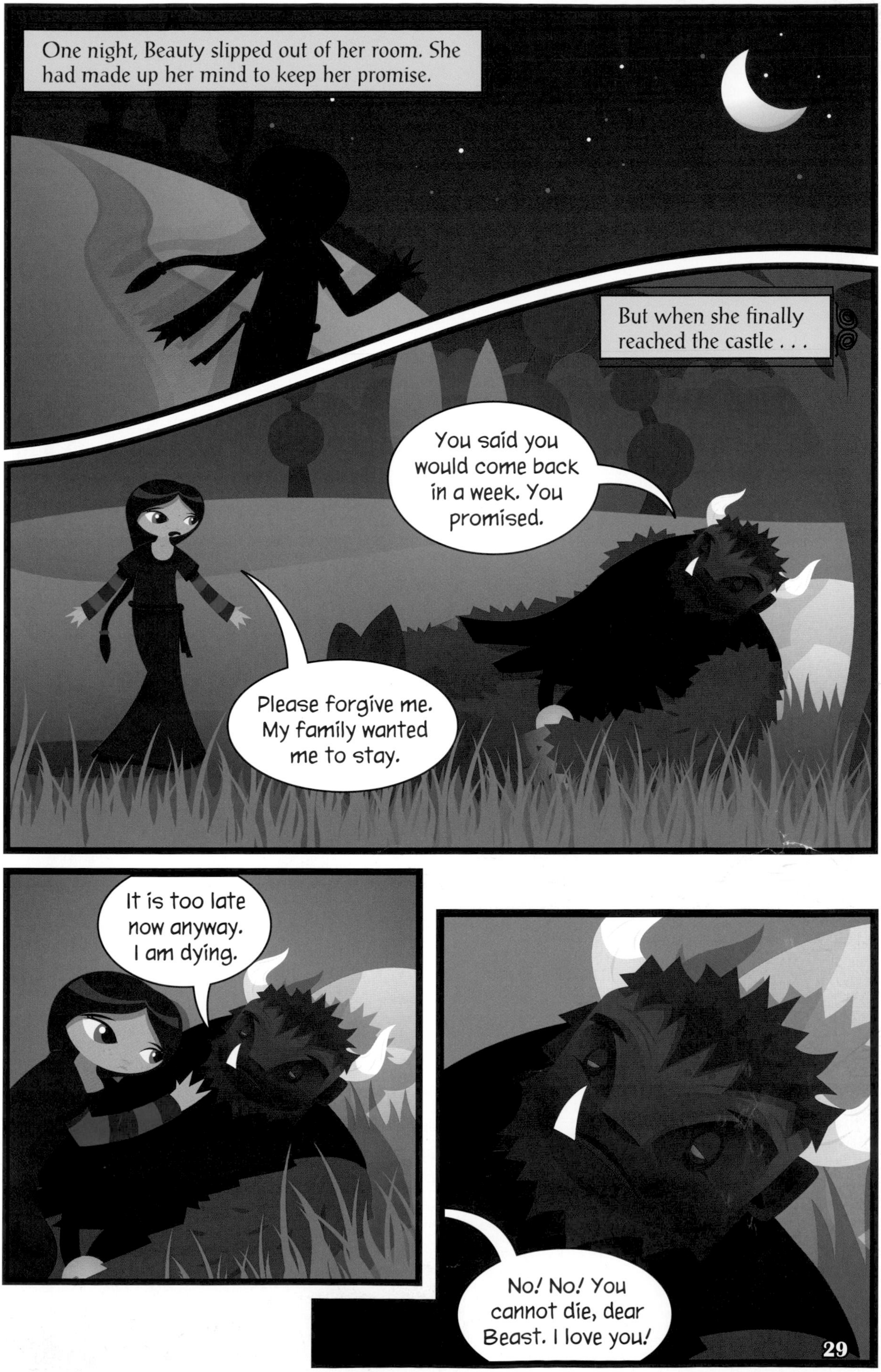
One night, Beauty slipped out of her room. She had made up her mind to keep her promise.
But when she finally reached the castle . . .
You said you would come back in a week. You promised.
Please forgive me. My family wanted me to stay.
It is too late now anyway. I am dying.
No! No! You cannot die, dear Beast. I love you!

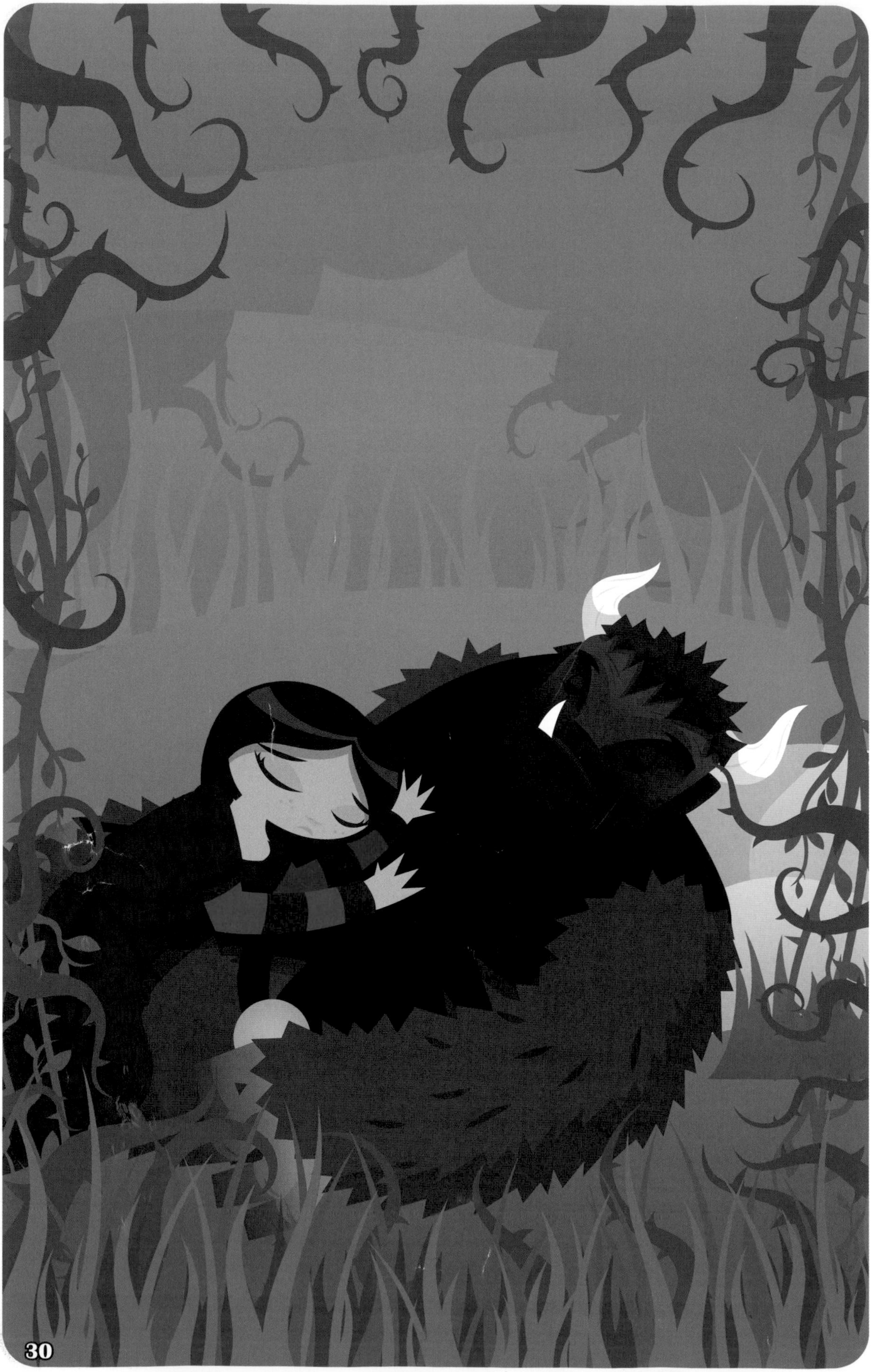

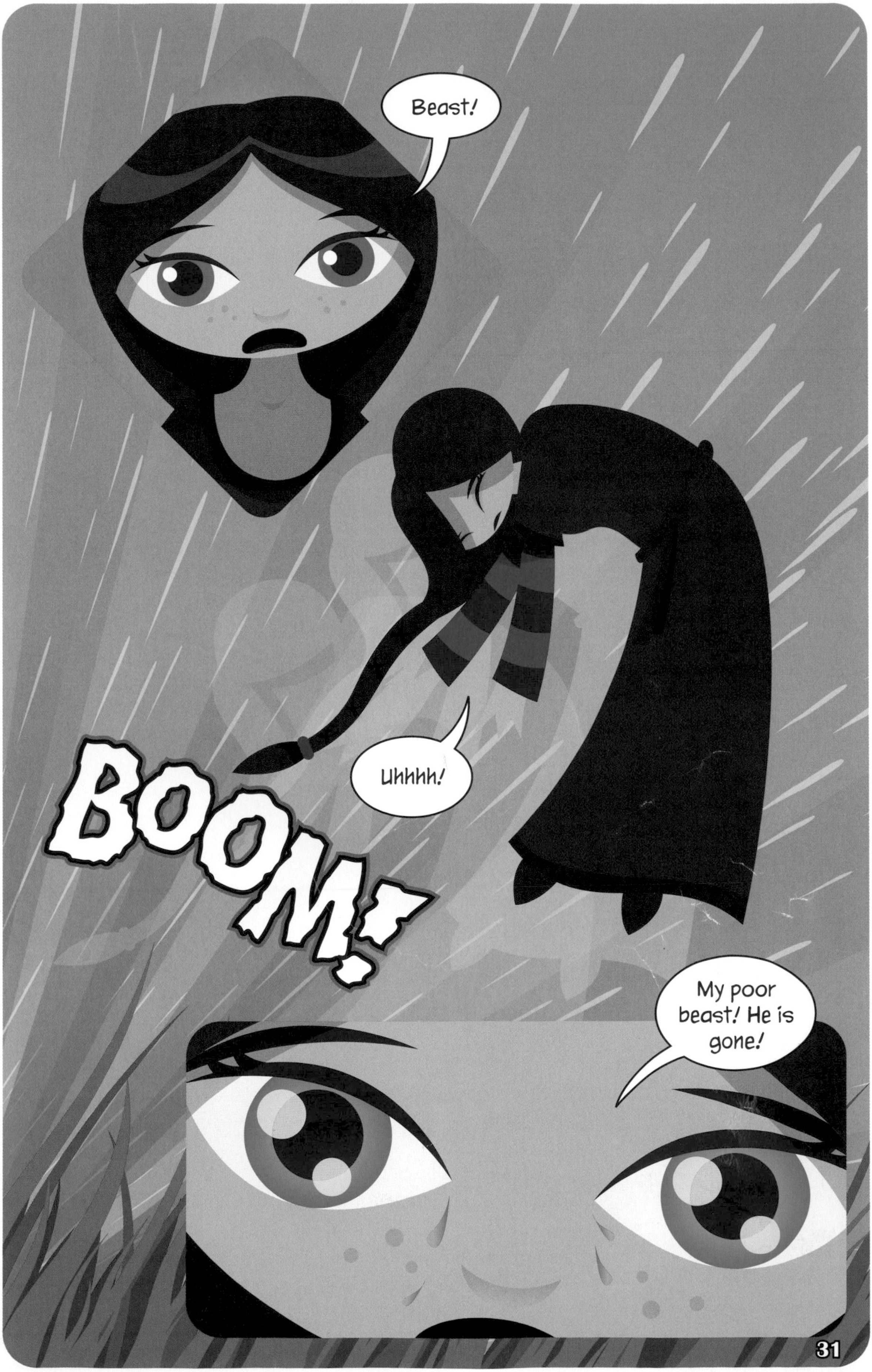
Beast!
Uhhhh!
BOOM!
My poor beast! He is gone!

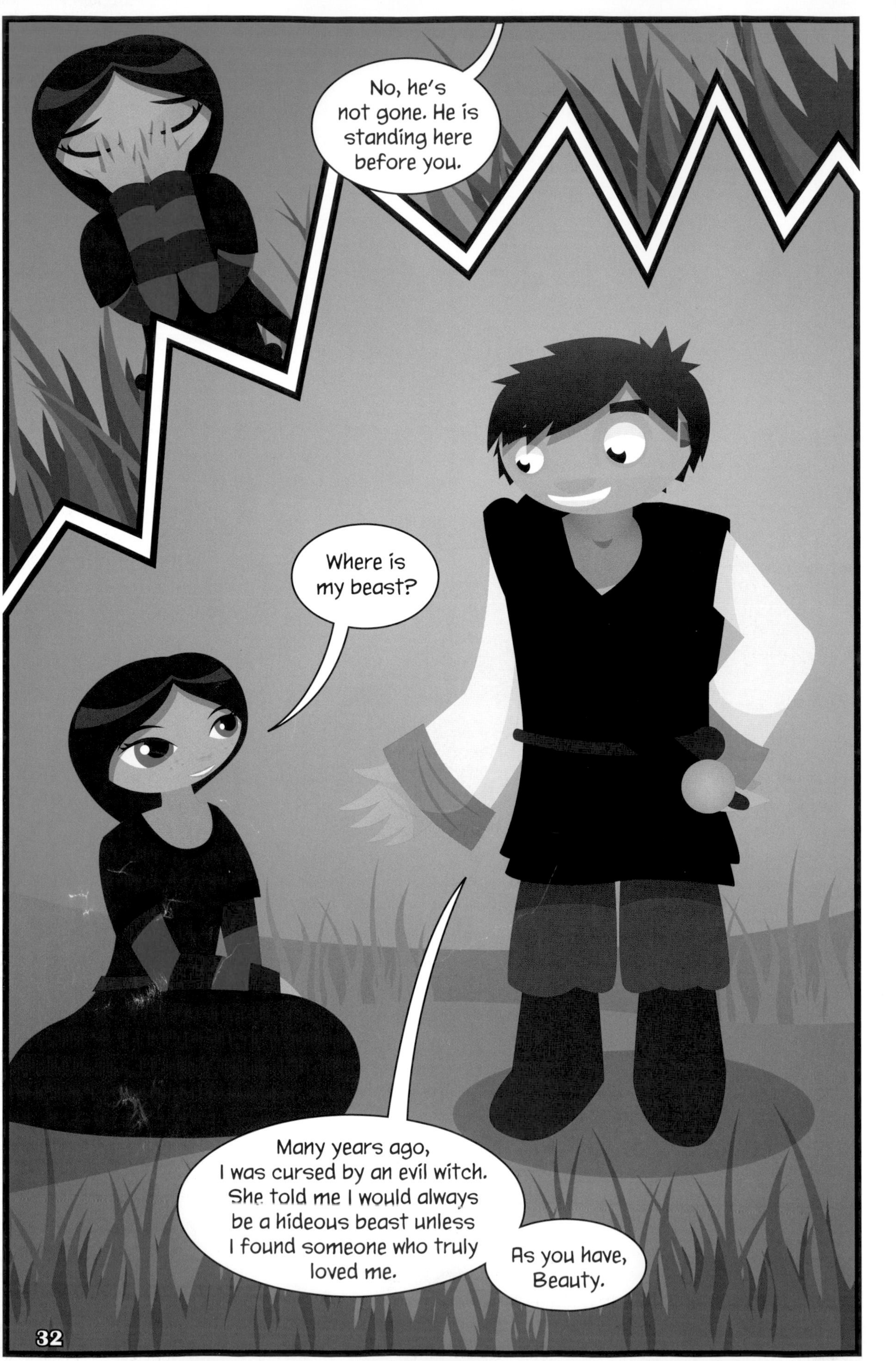
No, he's not gone. He is standing here before you.
Where is my beast?
Many years ago, I was cursed by an evil witch. She told me I would always be a hideous beast unless I found someone who truly loved me.
As you have, Beauty.

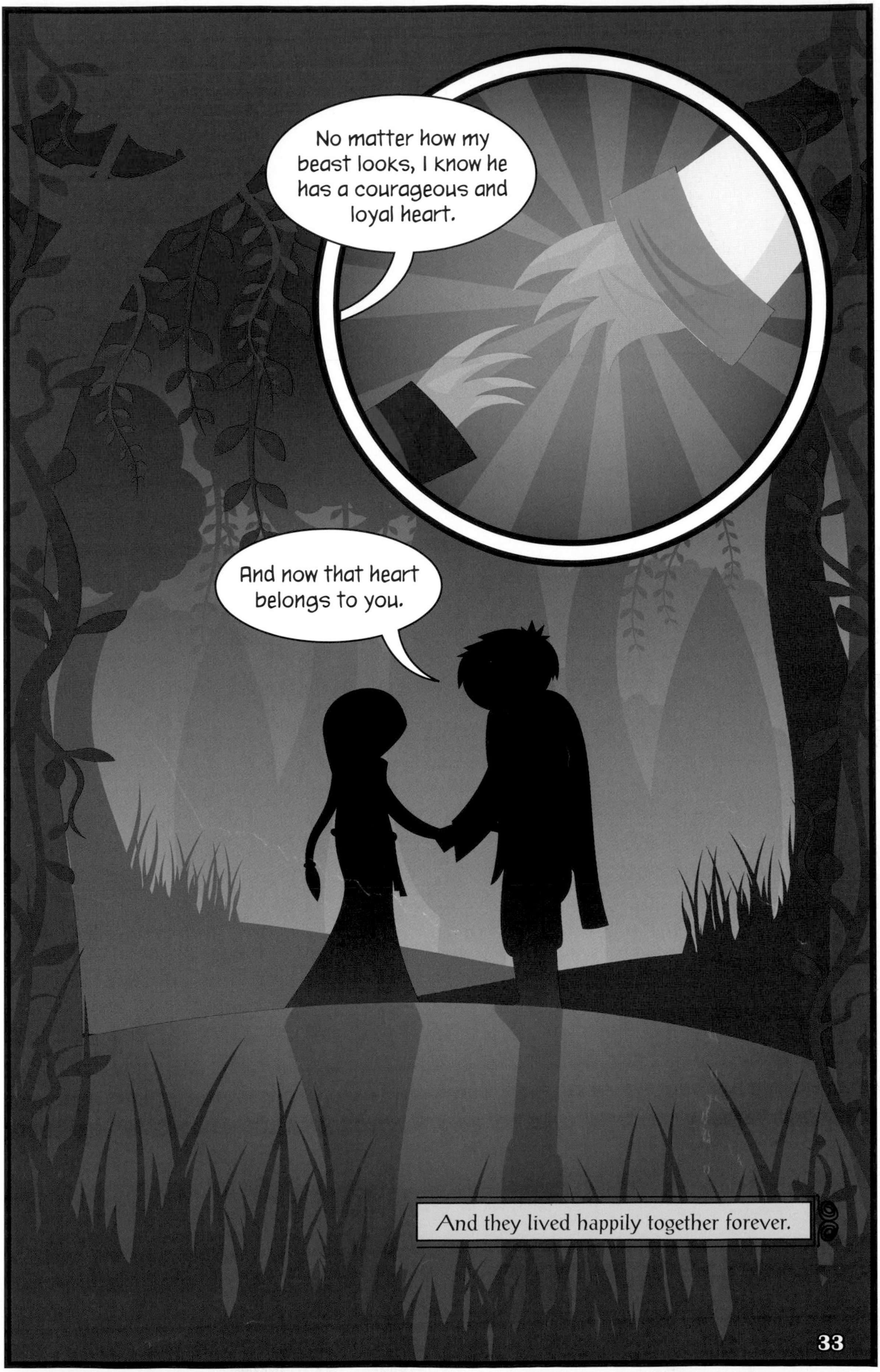
No matter how my beast looks, I know he has a courageous and loyal heart.
And now that heart belongs to you.
And they lived happily together forever.

ABOUT THE AUTHOR

Michael Dahl is the author of more than 100 books for children and young adults. He has twice won the AEP Distinguished Achievement Award for his nonfiction. His Finnegan Zwake mystery series was chosen by the Agatha Awards to be among the five best mystery books for children in 2002 and 2003. He collects books on poison and graveyards, and lives in a haunted house in Minneapolis, Minnesota.

ABOUT THE ILLUSTRATOR

Luke Feldman is an illustrator, animator, and designer from Australia. For more than 10 years, he has worked on high-profile projects for large corporations such as Microsoft and Coca Cola. He has also worked closely with the Australian education department, developing animations and interactive games for children.

GLOSSARY

carriage (KA-rij)—a vehicle with wheels, often pulled by horses

courageous (kur-RAY-juhss)—brave or fearless

demands (di-MANDZ)—asks for something firmly

described (di-SKRIBED)—created a picture of something in words

expensive (ek-SPEN-siv)—costing a lot of money

kindness (KINDE-ness)—if someone shows kindness, he or she is being friendly, helpful, and generous

loyal (LOI-uhl)—firm in supporting or faithful to one's country, family, friends, or beliefs

maiden (MAYD-uhn)—a young, unmarried woman

merchant (MUR-chuhnt)—someone who sells goods for profit

precious (PRESH-uhss)—rare and valuable

reunion (ree-YOON-yuhn)—a meeting between people who have not seen each other for a long time

tenderness (TEN-dur-ness)—if someone shows tenderness, he or she is being gentle or kind

THE HISTORY OF BEAUTY AND THE BEAST

The tale of BEAUTY AND THE BEAST begins hundreds of years ago. Even before it was first written down, the story had been passed from person to person for many generations.

Partly inspired by these oral tales, French author Madame Gabrielle de Villeneuve wrote the first-known version of BEAUTY AND THE BEAST in 1740. Villeneuve meant for her story to be read by adults rather than children. The novella, or medium-length story, was nearly as long as a novel. It contained many parts that were later taken out, including information about the beast's childhood. Possibly the biggest difference, however, comes at the end of Villeneuve's tale. In her version, the beast is never transformed back into a prince. This part of the story was added 16 years later.

In 1756, another French author named Madame Le Prince de Beaumont crafted the best-known version of the fairy tale. Beaumont's tale was much shorter than Villeneuve's story. It was also aimed at younger readers. The new version quickly became popular, and a year later the story had been translated from French to English.

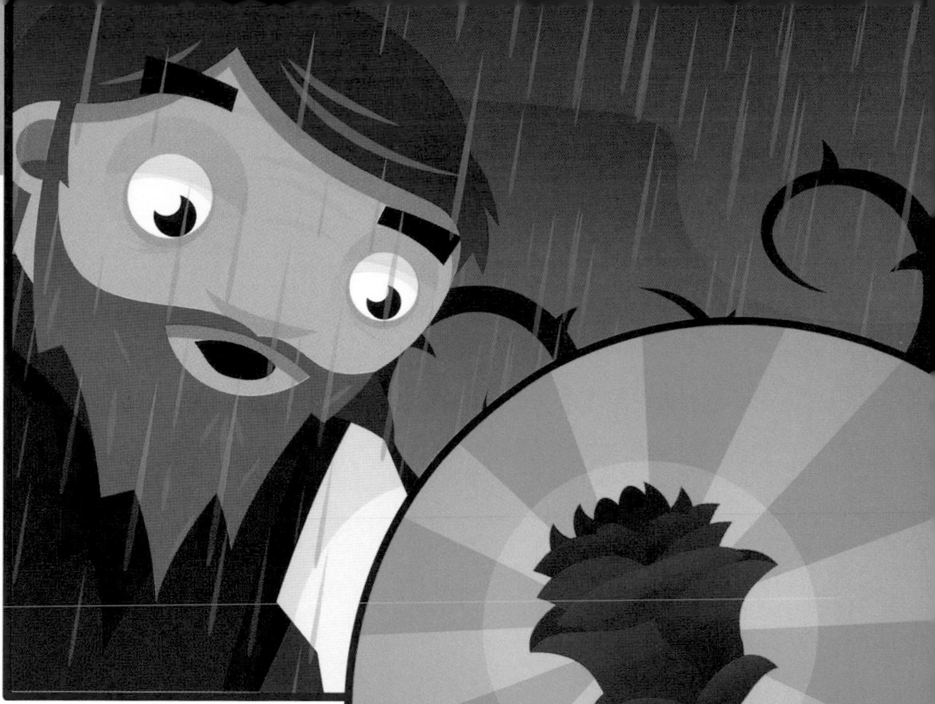

Since then, the story has been retold thousands of times in books, plays, and on film. On November 13, 1991, the Walt Disney Company released the animated version of **BEAUTY AND THE BEAST** to theaters. The film quickly became a success. It is the only animated picture to ever be nominated for the Academy Award for Best Picture.

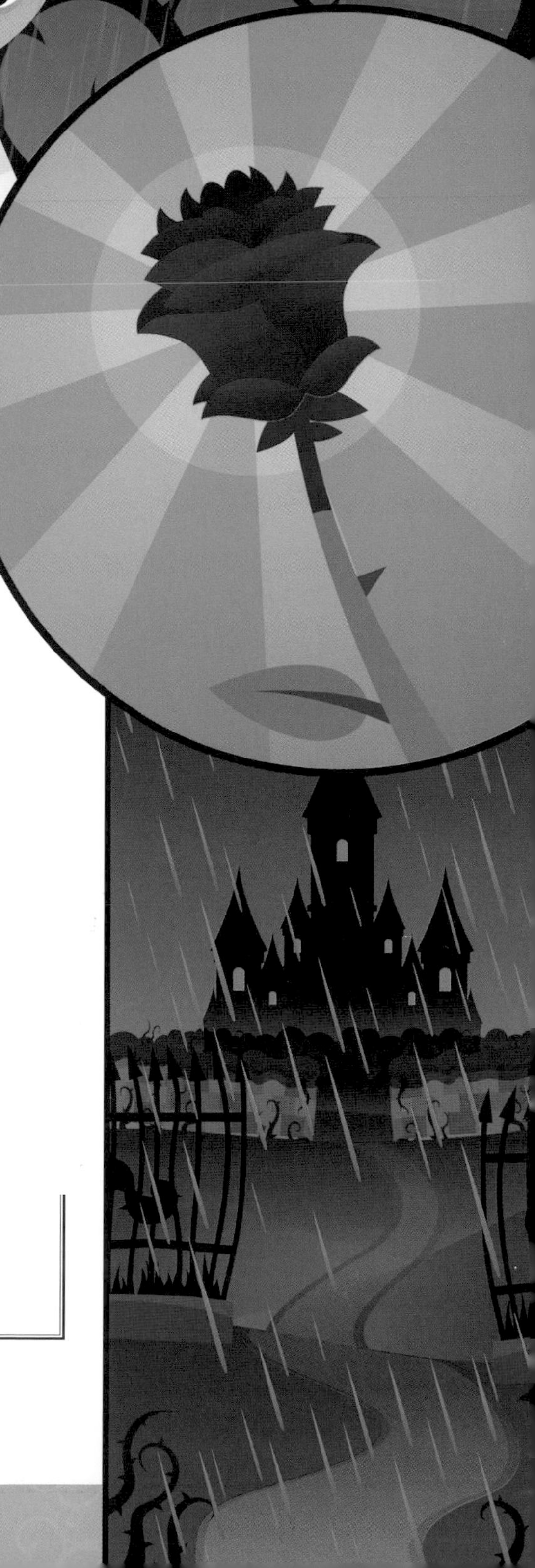

DISCUSSION QUESTIONS

1. Beauty's father asks his daughters what they would like him to bring back from his trip. Two of the daughters want dresses and jewels, but Beauty wants just one rose. What does this tell you about Beauty's character? What kind of person is she?

2. Beauty's family didn't want her to return to the Beast's castle. Why do you think Beauty chose to return anyway?

3. Fairy tales are often told over and over again. Have you heard the Beauty and the Beast fairy tale before? How is this version of the story different from other versions you've heard, seen, or read?

WRITING PROMPTS

1. Fairy tales are fantasy stories, often about wizards, goblins, giants, and fairies. Many fairy tales have a happy ending. Write your own fairy tale. Then, read it to a friend or family member.

2. Beauty's father said that his daughters could have anything they wished for. If you could have anything, what would it be? Describe why you made that choice.

3. The story says that Beauty and the Beast "live happily together forever." Write a story about their life together. Will they get married? Will Beauty's family come to live with them? Use your imagination.

INTERNET SITES

The book may be over, but the adventure is just beginning.

Do you want to read more about the subjects or ideas in this book? Want to play cool games or watch videos about the authors who write these books? Then go to FactHound. At *www.facthound.com*, you'll be able to do all that, and more. The FactHound website can also send you to other safe Internet sites.

CHECK IT OUT!